The Zook Family Revisited
Book Three

My Heart Cries Out
By
June Bryan Belfie

My Heart Cries Out

a novel
June Bryan Belfie

Chapter One
Lancaster County, Pennsylvania

The Zook's clapboard farmhouse was filled with well-wishers as family and friends gathered to celebrate the marriage of Kate Zook and Josiah Stoltz. People came from all over Lancaster County as well as Chester County in Pennsylvania and some as far as Ohio.

The scents of roast chicken and fresh-baked fruit pies filled the home as Amish women arranged platters of homemade food on the long tables. It was mild out for mid-December with only hints of the early blizzard showing along the shady side of the barn and house, so some of the younger people spent time outside, which helped with the crowding indoors.

The wedding ceremony was over too quickly. It was difficult to get an accurate account of guests, since some people arrived late and others left early, but at last count, Leroy figured more than a hundred and seventy-five people had attended his youngest daughter's wedding.

Leroy smiled over at his daughter, Katie, and her new husband, Josiah, who never left her side. He'd fought back tears at one point during the ceremony when they said their vows. It hadn't been that long ago that it was questionable if she'd ever marry, due to the existence of her leukemia. Never had life seemed more precious than when it looked like his darling child might not live to see old age, but the Lord had provided a way. It was discovered early, and thankfully, the medical profession had ways of treating it without resorting to chemotherapy.

Today, his Katie never stopped smiling. Yah, here was the Katie he'd known all her life. Sweet, pleasant—always ready with a kind word. She looked so lovely in her bright aquamarine dress, lovingly stitched by Mary, his dear wife.

He glanced over at Mary as she patted their middle daughter Ruthie's expanding tummy. Jah, it was her time again. Mary's excitement showed in her sparkling eyes. She never tired of greeting new grandchildren into the world. Even after raising six children, she looked young and energetic, though her bouts with bronchitis had caused her to lose more than ten pounds. He'd have to watch over her to make sure she got her proper rest. He couldn't take a chance on her becoming ill again.

Mary's mother sat in her wheelchair, beaming at her family. Goodness, she almost didn't make it. Thank God, she was finally making progress after her hip surgery. Dealing with surgery so soon after burying her husband, nearly caused the poor lady to give up, but here she was, enjoying her granddaughter's wonderful moment as she started her life with Josiah, a fine young Amish farmer.

"Leroy, why are you in the corner by yourself?" His friend, Toe, asked as he joined him with a plate full of homemade salads and cold cuts.

"Just thinkin' is all."

"Your Katie is a beautiful bride. Can't even tell she's been sick."

"Jah, that's what I was thinking myself. It's a miracle, for sure."

Toe grinned. "Now I have to get my youngest *maed* married off. Maybe we'll grab that young *sohn* of yours."

Leroy laughed. "Wayne ain't about to tie himself down. Lots of girls are trying to get his attention, but he fights em off."

"Chip off the ole block? Oh well, one of these days someone will catch his fancy."

Ruth leaned against her mother as Mary caught her husband's eye and motioned for him to join them. When he excused himself and made it over to her side, Ruthie announced it was her time to give birth. "I hate to leave, but my pains are getting real close. I'm not sure where Jeremiah went, *Daed*. He was with Mark. Have you seen him? Oh, here comes another pain, *Mamm*. I have to get out of here."

"Honey, you're not going anywhere. Lucky our midwife is here for the wedding. Let me go get her after you sit down."

Ruthie settled into a chair out of the way as Emma and Lizzy came over to check on her. "You're in labor?" Emma asked, concern written on her face.

"Oh, jah. *Und* how. Where's my husband?"

"We'll go upstairs, *schwester*. Lizzy, you look for Jeremiah. Where's Mamm?"

"Looking for Mrs. Horner."

"Oh, my, of all times. Should I tell Katie?"

"*Nee*, let her be. I don't want to spoil anything for her on her special day. Ooooh. I can't believe how fast it's coming."

"When did it start?"

"During the night, but I tried to ignore it."

"Ruthie! How can you possibly ignore birth pains?"

"It's not easy. There's Jeremiah, coming through the door. Thank God."

He made it over to her side in four strides. "Honey, I just saw your mamm. Is it true?"

"That I'm having a *boppli?* Oh, jah, it's a true statement, that's for sure. Help me get upstairs. Where's Nathanael?"

"With Hannah. He'll be fine. Let me help you."

A few of the guests realized what was transpiring and the women clustered around Ruthie while her mother searched for the mid-wife.

Belinda stood with her sister, Rachel, and watched the crowds of people as they enjoyed the festivities. If she left the Amish to marry, she would not have this kind of wedding – the only kind she knew. With friends and family rejoicing with you. Nee, it would probably be small and perhaps on the somber side. She dismissed her thoughts and talked to her older sister, Rachel, about her pregnancy. "You look gut, schwester. Not even showing much yet."

"It's too early to notice much. I feel okay, but I'm nervous. I'm afraid to have too much hope since losing our other boppli."

"I can imagine. But I've heard lots of women lose their first for some reason or other."

"I noticed Katie's brother, Wayne, looking at you, Belinda. I think he may have a crush on you."

"Jah, I think you're right, but I'm totally in love with Jeff. Besides, Katie's best friend likes Wayne. Has for years, so I'm no competition."

"I bet I know the girl. She keeps following him around. Guys don't like being chased. She should play hard to get and maybe he'd notice her more."

"Aren't you the worldly one," Belinda said, grinning at her sister.

Rachel blushed and giggled. "Nee, not worldly, but I listen to others talk. That girl is sweet looking. I'm surprised he's not interested."

"Katie said Becky, that's her name, has liked him forever, but she's ready to give up."

"I noticed the girl named Priscilla keeps flirting with him. She's pretty, but there's something I don't like about her. That's not nice of me to say…"

"Jah, Rachel. That's not like you to talk about someone, but I think it's because she seems full of herself. Like conceited. She was after Katie's husband for awhile, but he never gave her a second look. At least that's what he told Katie."

"I believe him. Look at the way he looks at his bride. Like she's the only one in the room. How sweet."

"It is. Katie is remarkable. She's handled her illness so well. Better than her mamm, I'm afraid. *Aenti* Mary's been real upset ever since she heard about the leukemia."

"The newlyweds are staying at the *dawdi haus*, aren't they?"

"Jah, Katie insisted, but just until Oma gets strong enough to take care of herself more. It's too much for Aenti Mary to do it alone and with all the boppli being born in the family, it leaves a lot on Katie's shoulders."

"Maybe they should put the lady in a nursing home."

"Aenti Mary won't hear of it."

"Who's that pretty English lady with the fancy clothes?"

"That's Aenti Esther from Philadelphia. The one Ruthie stayed with when she left Lancaster for awhile. She's a professor at a university."

"Wow. I bet she's real smart."

"And rich."

"Jah, I believe it. That dress wasn't made from two dollar a yard chintz."

"She's nice, Rachel. I'll introduce you later."

"Look over at Ruthie now. She's practically doubled over."

"Oh my, I wonder…"

"Jah, I bet. Of all times."

"Jah, that's the midwife helping her up the stairs. Goodness gracious, what a busy day.

Rachel laughed and shook her head. "You can say that again."

Chapter Two
Lancaster county, Pennsylvania

Mrs. Horner, the midwife, gave orders for fresh sheets, towels, and blankets to be laid out on the bed while she timed Ruth's contractions as she sat on a chair. Jeremiah held his wife's hand firmly and helped her onto the bed once it was prepared.

As things got closer, Mary and Jeremiah remained in the room, but Mrs. Horner suggested the others leave as Ruthie was struggling to keep herself in control. Too many people made the situation all the more difficult.

Nearly an hour passed and finally Emma and Lizzy, who stood just outside the door, heard the cry of the newborn.

Several minutes later, Mary came into the hall to announce the arrival of Daniel Fisher. "He weighed nearly seven pounds and my, he's a cutie. Mrs. Horner is cleaning him up and then we'll show him off."

"Wait till Katie finds out," Lizzy said with a wide grin.

"How's Ruthie doing, Mamm?" Emma asked.

"Real gut. She's strong, that girl. Made for boppli. Jeremiah looks a bit overwhelmed, though."

"Poor guy."

It wasn't long before Daniel was carried into the hall, by a very proud father, to be exposed to his new world. Jeremiah went downstairs and showed off his son. Katie nearly fainted when she saw him. "Oh, my, when did this happen? Where was I?"

"Enjoying your wedding party, I hope," Jeremiah said with an enormous grin.

"I can't believe it! Ruthie didn't even make a noise!"

"She's a brave girl, Katie. Just like you." Jeremiah handed the wrapped bundle with his newborn over to Katie. Daniel was sleeping, but his little mouth twitched and he moved his tiny fingers, fanning them into the air. Katie's eyes filled with unshed tears as she gazed upon this miracle. Oh, that one day she, too, would know the thrill of bringing a life into the world. There were no guarantees in life, of course, but her chances were slim according to the oncologist. Slim, but not totally negative. On this, she would rest and if she was unable to bear children, she was sure God would bring a young one into their lives who needed to be loved.

She kissed the top of his naked head and prayed a blessing over his young life. Then she handed him over to his father and touched Jeremiah's shoulder. "He's beautiful. I'm so happy for you."

People were surrounding the new baby now, most exclaiming shock at the sudden new arrival.

Josiah came over to the happy group and added his best wishes. He shook his head in wonderment as he expressed his surprise at seeing this event take place on his wedding day. "Ruthie pulled a gut one. And we had no idea," he added.

"Jah, she's a brave girl—never screamed or anything. I want to show Nathanael his new *brudder*, but I think Daniel's mama will be anxious to see her sohn back in her arms about now. Besides, I don't want him getting bad germs, and the little ones are clambering to see him."

Emma told him she'd bring Nathanael upstairs once she located him. He was playing blocks with several of the younger children in the kitchen when she spotted him. She took him by the hand and led him upstairs to his mother's bedside without telling him about his new brother. Ruth was holding the sleeping infant when her son arrived, wide-eyed. Jeremiah lifted him in his arms and then squatted next to the bed so he could touch his brother's hand.

"Remember, I told you about your mamm having a new boppli? Here he is, Nathanael. A boy like you, and we named him Daniel."

"He's funny looking," the toddler said, cocking his head to the side. "He got no hair."

"It will grow in," Ruth said smiling lovingly at her first born. "You didn't have much at that age either."

"Was I itsy-bitsy like him?" His eyes were round as saucers.

"Jah, pretty much."

"Okay, I gotta go now." He wiggled free from his father's arms and scooted back down the stairs to join his cousins and friends. Ruth smiled over at Jeremiah. "He seems so big now, in comparison."

"He does. Danki, Ruthie," he added as he leaned over and kissed her lips. "You make me so happy."

Ruth smiled at her husband. "We need to thank God, Jeremiah. He's blessed us so much."

"Jah, first bringing us together and now two wonderful-gut kinner. Let's pray together."

Ruth closed her eyes as her husband gave thanks to their maker. Another miracle. Another blessing. What a wonderful God.

Belinda and her family stayed with Gabe and Emma and their four children. When Belinda visited before to help with Oma's care, she stayed in the dawdi haus attached to the Zook's home, but now Katie and her new husband would be residing there—at least for a couple of weeks or months. Belinda knew Katie would prefer being in her own farmhouse with her new husband. Josiah had spent much time and money preparing their home, but he had understood and knew Katie's place was still at her parents' home, at least as long as Oma needed special care. As he had mentioned to Belinda, they would have their time together in their own home eventually. He hoped sooner rather than later and Belinda had nodded in agreement.

As the crowds left, Belinda and her whole family made their way over to Emma's, borrowing two buggies. The house was completely filled with folding cots and bedrolls as people prepared for the night. The next day they'd be returning to Ohio with their driver.

Belinda checked her pocket for her cell-phone, which Jeff had purchased for her when she was staying with the Zooks. She felt the hard surface of the phone and waited patiently while people used the bathroom and made their way to bed. Finally, she was alone in the bathroom to make her call to Jeff. How she wished he had been allowed to come to Pennsylvania for the wedding.

There was a time when her father had almost encouraged Jeff's visits, even though he was English, but no longer. Now they were forbidden to see each other. It wasn't fair. After all she was grown up now. She had a right to marry the man she loved. Just because he wasn't Amish, should she turn her back on him? Nee, there was no way she'd break off her engagement. Once in a while they managed to see each other, though sneaking out to see him caused her such guilt sometimes, that it took away the joy of being with him. He felt the same. He was a gut, honest man, and it hurt him as well to sneak around. But they were left with no choice.

She waited for him to answer the call. He picked up on the first ring. "Honey, I've been waiting all night."

"I'm sorry. This is the first opportunity I've had to call. It's been so busy."

"I hope you're having a good time. How was the wedding?"

"Lovely. Katie looked so pretty and you won't believe what happened." She proceeded to tell him all about Ruthie and the baby and then she described the food, the crowds, the service. They talked for nearly half an hour when she realized her battery was getting low. "I'd better hang up soon or I won't have enough power to talk to you tomorrow. I need to charge the phone in town when we get home."

"Belinda, I miss you so much. This is really hard not seeing you. I don't know how much longer I can live this way."

"I know. I know. I feel the same. We'll talk more when I get home. We'll have to see each other in a couple days or I'll go crazy."

"Me, too. Next time you call, we'll make arrangements to get together. We simply can't go on this way. Good night, my darling. I love you."

Belinda smiled into the phone. "And I, you. *Gutte nochte.*"

As she made her way down to the living room and her cot, she tiptoed past her younger sister, Nellie, who was snoring softly from her bedroll. After settling down, Belinda prayed for her whole family and she prayed for her parents to accept Jeff as a Mennonite and future son-in-law. God would have to work on their hearts.

Katie and Josiah were the last ones to retire. They went hand-in-hand into the dawdi haus. Mary had turned on some kero-lamps and there was a fire in the pot-bellied stove, which heated the whole building. There were two rooms and a small bath. Very adequate. The women had made Katie a beautiful quilt, which adorned the double bed.

Katie made her way into the bathroom to change her clothes and wash up. Her hand shook as she reached for her toothbrush. She took twice as long as usual to prepare for bed and when she made her way back to the bedroom, Josiah had already changed into a long white shirt and was sitting under the covers. She smiled timidly as she climbed into the other side of the bed and laid her head on the pillow.

"Hi, Mrs. Stoltz. Happy?" He lifted her head and put his arm under her.

She smiled up at him. "Oh jah. I sure am."

He leaned over and kissed her gently on her lips. "Tired?"

Her eyes filled as she nodded.

"You did so well to get through today, honey. It was exhausting."

"I had a wonderful day, though. I can't believe we're actually married."

He ran his other hand through her long hair. "You're very beautiful, Katie. Your hair is like silk."

He kissed her again and then laid back on his pillow. "You rest now. Try to sleep."

"But…"

"I know you're exhausted, Katie. You've been through so much—not just the wedding, but you know, all the other stuff."

"Leukemia? You can say it, Josiah."

"Okay, yah, the leukemia. We have the rest of our lives together, honey. Tonight it's more important for you to get your rest."

"You're so understanding." The tears rolled down her cheeks. "I want our time to be special and I am awful tired tonight."

"I know, honey. Please don't worry about it. When the time is right, then… In the meantime, I want you to get some sleep. If you're up to it, tomorrow, I'd like to take you over to our home, just to show you what I've done. It may not be too long before we're living there."

"I'd love to go over and see it again. I hope you're not too disappointed not to be in there yet."

"I understand completely, Katie-girl. This is cute here. We'll be just fine. I love your Oma. I can help, too, you know."

"I know, husband. She loves you too."

He continued to hold her in his arms and as she slept, he watched her slow gentle breathing. She seemed at peace with the world. The rays from the moon touched her fragile skin and it glowed in the silence of the night. He thanked God for his wife and prayed for her with all his heart.

Chapter Three
Lancaster County, Pennsylvania

Emma insisted on Belinda and her family staying an extra day before heading back to Ohio. Belinda hid her disappointment from her family. She missed Jeff so much, but there was nothing to be done about it. She'd make the most of her time with her extended family.

It was fun to spend time with everyone. Belinda loved being with Emma and Gabe's children, especially the twin girls, Deborah and Miriam. They seemed to remember her and gave her broad damp smiles as they chewed on their fingers and rattles. They each had cut their two lower front teeth and it made them all the more adorable in her eyes. At six months, they were attempting to sit up by themselves, but they needed to be surrounded by pillows when they sat on the floor.

It was a happy time for the Zooks. A wedding and a new baby—both at the same time.

Emma remarked about Oma's improvement with her health. "She beamed all day. It was so gut for her to be part of the events."

"It was. She looked younger even," Belinda's mother Grace said. "Katie looked gut, too, in spite of her illness. Mary said she was in remission. Thank the Lord for that."

"We've spent so much time in prayer, I think the gut Lord was sick of hearing us," Emma said smiling. Lizzy was sitting on the floor next to her mother listening.

"I ain't gonna stop now," she said looking up. "Now I have to pray that my schwesters cut more teeth soon. They drool all over me when I hold them."

Grace and her husband, Jed, laughed and Gabe joined in.

"That's what boppli do, young lady," he said as he joined his daughter on the floor. "What are you building here?"

"A hospital for my stuffed animals. I want to be a nurse someday."

Gabe looked up at Emma as his lips turned down. "Jah? Well, maybe not a real nurse, Lizzy. That takes a lot of schooling."

"I guess so. Okay, maybe I'll be a lady who helps with new babies. They learn from other people not from books and stuff."

"Jah, that would be better, little one," Gabe added.

Then he added several Lego's to one wall, as Jed squatted down to join them.

Emma handed one of the twins over to Belinda as she rose to start lunch. Grace reached for the other baby.

"Let's head over to Ruthie's later and check out the new boppli," Emma said to the group.

"I still can't believe how quickly everything happened," Belinda said as she snuggled the baby on her lap.

"Jah, that's the way she has her boppli. Real quick."

"She's fortunate. I hope I'm as lucky," Belinda added.

"Don't be in a rush for that, dochder," Grace said.

"So are you seeing anyone?" Emma asked.

Belinda shook her head. "I guess not."

"Guess? Don't you know?" Emma teased.

Grace broke in. "She ain't serious about anyone, but young Zeke's been over a few times. I think he has eyes for her."

"Mamm, please don't start about Zeke again. You know how I feel."

Lizzy looked up with innocent eyes. "I thought you loved that Englisher. Jeff something."

There was silence. It was deafening. Finally, Emma headed for the kitchen. "Hope everyone is hungry. Mamm made me bring a lot of food back yesterday from the wedding. I have enough potato salad for a hundred people."

Grace rose and carried Deborah into the kitchen where she joined Emma.

Belinda sat holding Miriam, as she stared into space. Her jaw was tense. Belinda felt her father's eyes on her and she returned his gaze. "What?"

"You have to give up the idea of Jeff. You know that. You can't break your mamm's heart."

"Not now, Daed. Please, let's wait until we're home.

Gabe cleared his throat and added another Lego to the roofline. "Time will heal, Belinda. You'll get over it."

She could feel her heart quicken. Mercy, she didn't want to get over it. She was going to marry Jeff, no matter what. Why did everyone act like she could just change her feelings like changing a frock? Surely, she wasn't the only one to know true love. She'd heard enough about Gabe and Emma's situation to know they overcame many obstacles before they married. It could be done. Besides, Jeff was planning to be Mennonite. In fact he already was. That should be close enough to the Amish to be acceptable. Goodness, why did everyone make so much fuss about the differences. Car – no car; electricity – no electricity; plain clothes – simple patterns. It all seemed so silly.

She heard her name called.

"Yah?" she turned toward the door to the kitchen.

"I wondered if you'd put Miriam down for a nap for me. She'll need a change, first," Emma said as she wiped her hands on a towel. "Your mamm is laying Deborah down for her nap at the same time."

"Sure. Do you want me to rock her first?"

"It shouldn't be necessary. She's overdue for her nap. She sometimes cries for a minute or two, but that's okay."

Belinda was glad for an excuse to leave the scene in the living room. If she spoke her mind right now, it would not be good. Why did Gabe get into it? It was like there was a conspiracy going on to ruin her life!

As she changed the diaper, she wondered about her own future. What would her children look like? Would they be as pleasant as these adorable girls? She certainly hoped so. Hopefully, Jeff would want as many as she did. It was always a dream of hers to have at least six children. She sighed as she laid the baby on her back and pulled the window shade.

After a loud wail, which caused Deborah to stir, Miriam rubbed her eyes and went off to sleep. Belinda took the opportunity to text Jeff about the delay in her return. He didn't text back. Was he upset? Perhaps he was working. She couldn't remember what his plans were, though with Christmas just around the corner, it was possible he was putting extra time in at his boss's small retail shop. He had opened it in November and so far sales had been sporadic. It meant more income for Jeff though, which was a good thing. He was conscientious about saving a little each paycheck.

Belinda decided she'd look for a baby-sitting job after the holidays. She had a friend who worked for an English family and made close to two hundred dollars a week. That would be wonderful-gut and she knew one of her English neighbors had recently had a new baby and wanted to return to work. She'd check there first.

Belinda's younger sister, Nellie, could handle the market with her mother. It wasn't all that busy this time of year. Besides, it was only one day a week. There just wasn't that much to do at home now. Besides, there was a strain now between her and her mother. Sometimes she even caught her mother with tears in her eyes. It was just too much sometimes to bear. Belinda's guilt even affected her sleep. Mercy, why did love have to be so difficult? It would have been easier if she'd fallen in love with an Amishman, that was for sure, but it didn't work out that way and it was too late to change her heart. Way too late.

When she arrived in the kitchen, the food was spread across the counters. There were cold-cuts, salads, and macaroni and cheese. Several desserts covered platters as well. Mervin, Gabe's oldest son, came in from the barn and joined his family for lunch. Nothing more was said about Jeff, much to Belinda's relief, and for a short time she allowed herself to think of something besides him, though her unanswered text tugged at the back of her mind. He always responded within minutes in the past. There was a good explanation, she was sure.

After changing plans with their driver, the family crowded together in two buggies and made their way over to the Zook's, where Ruth and her family remained due to the sudden birth of Daniel. The temperatures had dropped significantly overnight and the decision was made for them to remain for a couple more days so the family could help with Nathaniel, who was only sixteen-months-old and quite a handful.

Katie and her new husband were sitting on the sofa holding hands when Belinda arrived. Ruthie sat in the old rocker, holding the new infant while Mary and Oma sat on the loveseat opposite her. The rest of the men were outside tending to their chores when the new group arrived. It was wonderful to be among such a happy group and it was all the more poignant to Belinda as she considered the dreadful possibility of being shunned if she did marry outside her faith. It left her with a pit in her stomach. Surely, they wouldn't be so cruel. She caught her mother's eye and knew she was thinking the same thing. Lord, Jesus, please don't let that happen.

"Would you like to hold Daniel?" Ruth asked Belinda.

"Oh, I'd love to," she said, as she walked over and gently lifted the precious bundle into her arms. Then she and her mother, Grace, took seats on wooden straight chairs, which had been brought in from the dining room. Daniel grunted, eyes squeezed shut, and his tummy gurgled. Belinda touched his soft cheek and marveled at the perfection of this new child. God was so amazing. Oh, that she would be blessed with a son like him someday. Why did tears rise suddenly? Why was everything so heartrending now? Each family event became more engraved in her mind and heart, perhaps because her once secure life was now threatened. It wasn't right. Surely love shouldn't cause so much pain.

"Honey, what's wrong?" Belinda heard her mother's voice, but she looked down at the baby, embarrassed by her show of emotions.

"It's okay. Nothing's wrong. I'm just affected by seeing Daniel. He's so tiny and dear."

"Jah, and perfect. It is wonderful-gut," Grace remarked, nodding at her daughter.

Ruth smiled at Grace. "Gott has been gut, that's for sure."

"How does big brudder, Nathaniel, feel about sharing you now?" Grace asked.

Ruth laughed and shook her head. "He's too busy to care much at this point. I'm sure they'll be gut friends someday though when Daniel can throw a ball."

Belinda wiped her eyes with one sleeve and made an effort to smile. "Does Daniel keep you awake much, Aenti Ruth?"

"Oh jah. I slept in kitten naps all night. Never soundly. My husband made up for it. He snored half the night."

The women laughed. Josiah, who had been silent, grinned. "I'm sure I wouldn't be able to sleep a wink."

Katie looked over at him and pictured him holding a son of his own. Dear God, would it ever be so?

Oma wanted to hold Daniel before going in for her nap, so Belinda settled him into her arms and kissed the side of Oma's head. Oma grinned up at her. "My angel returned. You look so gut, Belinda. I hope you're happy."

"Jah, as happy as I can be under the circumstances."

"Oh, circumstances. Jah, they can affect you for sure. I'm happy, too, considering everything that hurts my heart."

"Now Mamm, don't think negative," Mary said as she moved closer to her mother to help support the infant.

"I have Daniel safe, Mary. I ain't about to drop him."

"I know, Mamm. Just in case—I want to be here."

Oma rolled her eyes and everyone tried to hold back laughing, but Ruthie giggled out loud. "He sure doesn't weigh much yet. He's strong though. Even stronger than Nathanael was when he was born. You should feel him grip your finger."

Oma moved her free hand and tucked her index finger under the baby's open hand. He immediately embraced it and held on tightly. "Goodness me, he is strong! He'll be farming with his daed before you know it."

Wayne came into the living room and nodded to everyone, his eyes settling on Belinda's for an extra couple of seconds.

"Daed wants to know if you need him to slaughter some chickens for tonight," he said to his mother.

Mary shook her head. "Nee, it's all taken care of. I made a huge rabbit stew earlier. Tell you're daed to leave those poor chickens alone. I want them as stewers and they're too young yet."

Wayne walked over to Oma's chair and grinned down at the baby. "He's cute for a boppli. I bet I looked like him. Did I Mamm?"

Mary smiled at her handsome teen-age son. "Jah you did, sohn. You were a sweetie-pie just like him."

Belinda noticed his skin flush bright red at his mother's remark.

Katie mentioned that Becky was coming over later in the day and with that, Wayne retreated to the outdoors. Grace remarked about how tall he had gotten and what a good catch he'd be for a young woman. She glanced over at Belinda, who totally ignored the comment.

"I think he likes my friend, Becky," Katie said. "They're spending more time together."

"That's nice, Kate. I hope it works out for them," Belinda added, hoping her voice sounded as sincere as she meant it to be. If it hadn't been for Jeff, perhaps she wouldn't be so encouraging about his relationship with Becky, but her eyes were for only one young man now.

The day was wonderful. Laughter and love filled the homestead and the chill in the air could not detract from the warmth in the simple clapboard farmhouse.

Chapter Four
Holmes County, Ohio

The ride back to Ohio seemed endless. Belinda had not heard back from Jeff and now her cell phone battery was dead. How would they get in touch? She might have to go to the shop where he worked, but it meant lying to her parents. She had hoped lying was a thing of the past, but unfortunately the only way they could correspond, which was forbidden, was by meeting secretly. Maybe the time would pass more quickly if she got the job. At least her mind would be occupied by something other than Jeff. It was taking its toll on her. She not only didn't sleep well, she felt downright cranky sometimes, and found it difficult to be pleasant to those around her.

During the ride, the rest of the family chatted amicably about their visit, exclaiming amusement at the children's antics and going over the wedding and the reception in detail. Belinda stared out the side window of the van and watched the landscape race past her. Things seemed so hurried from the inside of an automobile, so unlike the pleasant, cloppity-clop of the family horse as he trotted along the country roads. There was time to observe the small things in life from that perspective—the wild flowers alongside the road, the chattering squirrels and stalking cats, the occasional hawk soaring toward a tidbit. All the things of nature that were imbedded in her mind and memory.

Funny, she didn't need photos. It was all right there in her head waiting to be retrieved at will. Even faces. She never forgot a face of a friend or family member. She could recall every little thing—colors, imperfections, even stray hairs. When she thought about it, she didn't need much of anything to make her happy.

How fortunate to be raised in a loving home. She heard about the millions of children raised in single family homes or on the streets fending for themselves. It seemed so remote. That wasn't her world. She couldn't even conjure up in her mind life being that difficult—so different from her own. Her heart went out to those strangers, but it was almost like fiction.

Her world was predictable in comparison. Of course, there were the unexpected illnesses and accidents, the occasional disappointments; but as a woman, she knew what was expected of her. She would be the glue in her future family. The one who provided a safe haven for her loved ones. A home with nourishing meals, laundered clothing, children cared for and loved. A place where her hard-working husband could retreat to and know he was respected. In return she would be protected and cherished and provided for. This is the way it was. It always had been—it always would be.

Or would it?

The voice of their driver interrupted her thoughts. He asked if anyone needed to use public facilities since he was approaching a rest stop. No one did, so he continued on and she returned to her thoughts. This time she tried to picture her life with Jeff as a Mennonite wife. There were pluses. They would have a car, most likely, and it would have heat in the winter and air-conditioning in the summer. Just like their house. Jah, big pluses. And a home with a furnace and electric lights from a switch. Her clothes would be more modern. Brighter colors and even some sweet prints. They could hang pictures in their house and even take photos of their boppli. My, it sounded pretty gut.

But where did her family fit in? When would they ever come by? Would they be allowed? The church service wouldn't be in the familiar language of her forefathers. The sings would be ever so different. And Mamm and Daed. How often would she see them? Would her friends still be there for her? She'd have Carrie, of course. Jeff's sister was a sweetheart and they'd be like real schwesters. But what about Rachel? And dear sweet Nellie? Oh, how that would affect her younger sister. They'd always been close. And Gideon. His wonderful grin—his hearty laugh. *Oh, Jeff, please become Amish.*

At last they reached the house and her father paid the driver, while Gideon reached for their suitcase and travel bags. Rachel walked ahead with her husband, Reuben, and Nellie put her arm around Belinda as they headed toward the back door. "Did you have fun?" she asked.

"I did. How about you?"

"It was ever so much fun. I love everyone. That new boppli is the cutest thing I ever saw. I let him grab my finger once. It was neat."

Belinda placed her arm around her sister's shoulder. "How many boppli do you want someday?"

"A dozen. And a year apart so they'll be close friends."

"Whoa! You're gonna be a busy girl!"

"You'll help me out. And so will Rachel. We're gonna all live as neighbors."

"So you have it all figured out already."

"Jah. I even have names picked out."

"Hey, get the door for me," Gideon called over as he stood with arms filled.

"I got it," Rachel said as she reached under the rock for the spare key.

Belinda had a flood of memories when she saw the key being placed in the lock. How many times had she used it when she'd sneaked off in the evenings to be with her English friends? A fresh wave of guilt washed over her. Oh, well, that was a thing of the past. Of course now with Jeff...but that's different. After all she and Jeff were in love and so nothing else counts. Was she lying to herself or did she truly believe her rationalization?

Grace followed her daughters and entered the house.

"Mamm, the fire went out. It's freezing in here," Nellie said as she opened the grate to the coal stove.

"Your daed will get it going again, quick as a hare. Just leave your woolen jacket on till it warms up."

Belinda rubbed her hands together and placed them in her coat pockets.

When Jed came in, he was carrying some kindling with him. After plunking down all the packages, Gideon went out to retrieve a few split logs for his father. They worked like a team. It was hardly necessary to discuss things, as they seemed to read each other's minds.

Belinda unwrapped a loaf of white bread leftover from the wedding and proceeded to cut it into slices, laying them on a clean plate. Rachel brought out a jar of homemade strawberry jam and Nellie set the table with plates and silverware. Grace opened a jar of pickled zucchini from the summer and cut up some smoked sausage. Within minutes the table was filled with nourishing food as Nellie poured milk into glasses and added homemade potato chips—her favorite food.

After they ate, as they were cleaning up, a car could be heard coming down the drive. Belinda looked out and watched as Carrie climbed out the driver's seat with a bag in her hand. She was alone, but she was a welcome sight. At least to Belinda.

When she got to the door, Belinda opened it and invited her in. Nellie smiled and greeted her. Grace looked none too happy, though she managed to say hello.

Carrie placed the bag, which was filled with donuts from the market on a counter, and then Belinda led her friend into the living room where they'd have a degree of privacy.

"It's good to see you," Carrie began. "Listen, while I'm able, here's a note from Jeff. He mislaid his phone yesterday and then when he did find it, he tried to call you, but got no answer."

"Jah, my phone died. Danki. Is he okay?" Belinda asked as she tucked the paper into her apron pocket.

"He's been super busy, but he said to give you a hug for him. So here it is."

She leaned over and squeezed Belinda, who hugged her back.

"I miss him so much," Belinda said, her voice tremulous.

"But you had a nice time in Pennsylvania anyway? How was the wedding? And Katie, how did she look?"

"It was real nice. Katie looked wonderful. She smiled the whole day, but I could tell she was tired by evening. She kept yawning. It was fun to be there, but I would have preferred it, if Jeff had been with me."

"Of course. I understand. He's working lots of hours. He should be able to save some money anyway."

"That's the hope. I'm going to look for a baby-sitting job. I need to get busier. Winters can drag."

"Good idea. If you want me to, I'll ask around."

"I'll let you know. I have a neighbor who I heard might be looking for a sitter. She and her husband are lawyers in Lancaster and she wants to get back to work soon."

"How old are her kids?"

"I think she only has one boppli. A baby girl."

"That would be simple then. Well, maybe not 'simple' but you know what I mean."

"Sure, easier than six little ones. Carrie, do you think Jeff really misses me?" Belinda asked as she motioned to the sofa where the girls sat down next to each other.

"Oh, yeah. He mopes around the house like he's under anesthesia. Dad's annoyed sometimes. It's a bit of strain on everyone. My parents have not made things easy on Jeff about the Mennonite thing. They've tried to convince him to give up some of his ideas and concentrate on going to a four-year college."

"Dear me, that would put our wedding off even longer."

Carrie twisted a long strand of hair and looked over at Belinda. "I'm dating a new guy."

"Really? No more Dan?"

"No more Dan. He's a loser. This guy is someone you'd approve of. He's a Mennonite friend of Jeff's."

"What's his name?"

"Randy Davidson."

"I think I met him once. Black wavy hair? Not too tall?"

"That's him. He's not handsome or anything, but he's so nice to me. So respectful."

"I'm happy for you, Carrie, but what about your folks? Do they know you're dating someone plain?"

"I usually see him at the meeting house or I go with Jeff and we hang out. It's not serious or anything. He hasn't even tried to kiss me yet."

Belinda giggled. "I would hope not."

"Belinda, in my world that's rare."

"Jah, I know. I found that out pretty quick. It was scary."

"I think I like it better when a guy waits awhile. It's more special that way. Jeff told me some of the Mennonite guys wait until they propose to ask for a kiss."

"So sweet. Too late I guess for me."

"Randy's so funny. He loves to joke around with me. We have so much fun together."

"And you don't have to worry about him coming on too strong, like with Dan."

"It is refreshing," she said, nodding. "I wish you had pictures of the wedding. You could have taken some with your cell phone, if you'd been careful not to be seen."

"I wouldn't dare. Besides, the stupid thing was running low. I don't know how I'm going to recharge it. I run out of excuses about getting to town and all."

"Maybe I can pick up a battery charger for you."

"Do they have them?"

"I don't really know, but I'll look into it. I guess that wouldn't work, cause you'd need to plug in the re-charger. Oh well." She nearly whispered now. "Do you think you should read the letter in case you want to send word back to my brother?"

"Maybe. Okay." Belinda took out the letter and read to herself.

Dear Belinda,

It seems like forever since we've seen each other. This whole deception thing is driving me nuts. We have to talk and soon. Carrie will bring back word of when we can meet. Please think of someway to make it to town tomorrow. I have off most of the day. I'll work it so I can meet you at your convenience. We can meet at the library if you want or the ice cream shop. (I bet I know what you'll pick. LOL)

I love you, sweetheart and I miss you with all my heart.
Jeff

"Oh, Carrie, I can't wait. Okay, tell him I'll make it to town by noon tomorrow. We can meet at the ice cream shop. I don't know what excuse I'll use, but I'll work something out."

"And if you can't? Will you be able to let him know somehow?"

Belinda let out a long slow breath. "Nee. I'll be there, that's all."

Nellie popped through the door from the kitchen. "Hey, wanna play Monopoly?"

"I have to be going, Nell," Carrie said as she stood up. "Maybe next time."

"You just got here."

"I know, but I'm going to see a friend soon."

"Too bad. Oh, well, will you play, Belinda?"

"Not now, Nellie. I haven't even unpacked yet."

"Wow. That should take all of two minutes."

"Ha. Ha. Maybe I'll play rummy later. Monopoly takes too long, unless Gideon wants to play, too."

"I'll ask, but you know him. It's all 'kid-stuff' now that he's such a *big man*."

The girls laughed and Belinda grabbed her shawl to go out to the car with Carrie. Nellie followed them out. Belinda's spy was back.

Chapter Five
Lancaster County, Pennsylvania

Leroy and his son Wayne removed the few remaining benches from the porch and living room—reminders of the joyful wedding day. Josiah pushed the furniture back into place and wiped down spills on the kitchen linoleum, in spite of protests from Katie and her mother, who considered that to be a woman's job.

While this discussion took place, Katie dried the few remaining platters and placed them in the proper cabinets.

Mary looked around and nodded approval as the family worked as a team to put the house in order. She heard her mother call to her and went into her room to attend to her needs.

Oma sat on the edge of her bed, dangling her feet. "What's all the ruckus out there, Mary? I thought you had cleaned up yesterday."

"There's always more to be done, Mamm, you know that. Do you need to use the bathroom?"

"Not yet. I just hate missing all the activity. Maybe I should come into the kitchen now."

"Let's wait until the floor dries completely. Josiah wiped it down for us. We don't need you falling again."

"Ach. Don't bring that up again. I'm ever so much stronger now."

Mary smiled at her mother as she reached for a brush. "See? You had fun being at the wedding. You wouldn't have wanted to miss it."

"And the new boppli. My, what a day it was. Too bad Esther had to leave right away."

"At least she made it. I feel closer to my schwester all the time."

"That's a song to my ears, *dochder*. Families have to remain close. It's been far too many years without contact with my Essie. Time wasted."

Mary nodded. She brushed her mother's long white hair, untangling the few knots as she worked. Then she twisted it into a braid and arranged it under a fresh kapp. She stood back and smiled. "You look pretty as can be."

Her mother let out a giggle. "Goodness, a crinkled up old lady? Pretty? Go check the floor. Maybe it's dry now."

Katie came in with folded sheets in her arms. "Oma, you look ready for a party and it's only nine in the morning. You're usually just waking up."

"Too much going on around here."

Mary smiled over at Katie. "Jah, your *grossmammi's* afraid she'll miss something. Is the floor dry yet?"

"Jah, Josiah dried it down with old towels so no one would slip."

"My, my. You found yourself quite a husband," Oma said, grinning at her granddaughter.

"That I did, Oma. He's wonderful-gut. God has blessed me."

"Come give me a kiss. Now that you're a matron, you'll have less time for me."

Katie laid the linens aside and sat on the bed next to her grandmother, who remained seated on the edge. She put her arms around the woman and they shared a sweet moment as Katie kissed her soft cheek. "I'm so glad you were present at our wedding, Oma. It would not have been the same without you."

Oma's eyes filled. "I'm just sorry my dear husband wasn't here too, but I'll tell him all about it when I see him in heaven."

"Let's just hope that is a long time from now," Mary added as she pulled her mother's wheelchair next to the bed and locked the wheels. "You must be hungry, Mamm. I made extra blueberry pancakes this morning. Your favorite."

"I thought I smelled pancakes. Are they still hot?"

"I set some aside for you and they're sitting in the oven."

"Mary, you think of everything. Gott bless you."

While Oma sat at the side of the table eating, Katie and Josiah joined her and sipped their fresh-brewed coffee. Josiah placed his hand over Katie's and smiled. "Your Mamm said she'll take care of things here so we can go look at the house together. Are you up to it?"

"Of course. I admit, I'm still worn out from the wedding, but I'm anxious to see the house again. We can take some of our gifts over."

"Be sure you take the dishes Aunt Esther gave you," Mary said. "She bought twelve place settings. That must have cost her a pretty penny."

"Mamm, she also gave us money."

"Oh, my."

"Five hundred dollars!"

"My goodness! I can't believe it." She clucked her tongue. "She's too generous."

Oma nodded. "She's a rich lady now. She just wants to share it with her family."

"What else do you want to take over, Katie? The pans the Yoders gave you?" Mary asked.

"I think everything that goes into the kitchen would be nice. Will you manage if we stay most of the day, Mamm?"

"Oh mercy yes. Hannah's coming by to help me with the bath later."

"I don't need a bath," Oma stated, wrapping her arms across her chest. "I hate getting all wet. Just wipe me down, dochder."

"Mamm, you know it's better to soak."

"It's silly. It tires me out too much."

"Well, we'll see, Mamm. Please don't worry about it."

A while later, Josiah and Katie headed over to their house, their buggy filled with cartons of gifts. Katie was excited as they turned down their drive and pulled behind the kitchen door.

"Wait here, Katie. I have to do something." Josiah unlocked the door and disappeared inside for a couple minutes. Then he returned and opened the buggy door for Kate, extending his arms. When she set her boots on the ground, he swept her into his arms.

"Josiah, what on earth?"

"I'm gonna do an English tradition, Katie-girl. Just don't tell." He carried her up the two steps to the small back porch and pushed the door open with his foot. Then he took her over the threshold and set her on her feet again.

Katie giggled. "After all that food I ate, I'm surprised you can lift me."

"You're light as a kitten." He drew her close and kissed her—a lingering, tender kiss. "I love you, Mrs. Stoltz."

"Oh, Josiah, I'm so happy I could burst."

"We're alone for the first time."

"Jah. I know."

"There's not a soul around."

Katie felt a blush rise on her cheeks. "Not a living soul."

"We don't have to go back for several hours."

"Nee. You're right."

"Do you want to rest awhile?"

"I don't need to, Josiah. I'm feeling ever so gut."

"Gut enough to…?" His tender eyes met hers.

"Jah." Katie reached up and took his face in her hands and drew his lips to hers. They held each other in silence as Katie felt his lips move to her cheek.

Then before she knew what was happening, he lifted her in his arms again and was headed up the staircase. She closed her eyes as she felt his strong embrace and then found herself on their marriage bed. Slowly and gently, Josiah removed her kapp, undid her braided hair and smoothed her long tresses against the fresh pillowcase.

"You are Gott's blessing to me, Katie-girl. I never want to do anything to hurt you. You must promise to always speak truth to me."

"I will, Josiah, and I want to be yours. Your helpmate and your wife."

"You are my beloved."

And two became one, as it is written.

Later they unwrapped all the gifts and worked together to set up their home. They placed some of the colorful dishes on a shelf and Katie added bright yellow placemats to their kitchen table.

It was nearly four by the time they returned. Hannah had already left. Oma was resting from her bath, Mary had supper nearly ready, and Leroy and Wayne were playing checkers near the coal stove. The smell of baked meatloaf with onions permeated the room. In spite of all the pleasant sounds and smells, Katie knew it would soon be time to leave the safety of her parents' home and set up housekeeping with her dear husband. She would not rush it. As of now, she was where she needed to be. Others always came first to Katie. That was the Amish way.

Chapter Six
Holmes County, Ohio

Belinda sat at a small round marble-topped table for two as she watched the pretty young clerk stack three scoops of strawberry ice cream on a sugar cone and hand it to a customer. The young mother then handed the cone to an adolescent boy with freckles and they headed toward the door.

Her own dish, which had contained one scoop of chocolate, sat nearly empty as she fiddled with her spoon, swirling the melted cream about. Two other couples came in and were waited on.

Where was Jeff? He was supposed to meet her half an hour ago. Surely he hadn't forgotten. Could he have been in an accident? Just when she was considering her options, she saw him through the glass door as he approached the entrance to the ice cream shop.

He came directly to her side and apologized. "Of all days, I had a customer who purchased over four hundred dollars worth of stuff and of course, I didn't have the right cartons for everything. It was a nightmare."

"It's okay. I was beginning to worry."

"I tried to call you…"

"My phone is still dead."

"I figured. We'll get it charged. Maybe we can plug it in here while we eat. I'll check with Sue."

"Sue?"

"The girl who works here. I used to go to school with her. Did you eat already?" He looked at her empty bowl with a slight frown.

"I had to do something while I waited."

"Want another scoop or a cone?"

"Nee, I'll just wait with you."

As he walked over to the counter, Sue smiled at him and they chatted for a minute before he gave her his order.

Belinda felt disappointed in their greeting. He had seemed pre-occupied and had barely looked at her. Now he seemed happier to talk to that Sue girl.

When he returned, Belinda sipped from her water glass and looked down at the table.

"What's wrong, Belinda? Are you mad I was late?"

"Nee. I understand."

"Did you enjoy your time with the family in Pennsylvania?"

"It was fun. I told you already on the phone."

They sat silently for a moment while he spooned a large amount of ice cream into his mouth. "They make the best."

"Jah, almost as gut as Mamm's."

"I forgot. You're right. But for a shop—"

"Jah, it's pretty gut." He hadn't even touched her. Not even with his hand. Nothing.

"Boy, has it been busy lately. It's hard to catch my breath. With Christmas coming, the shop has been doing really well."

"I'm glad." What did she care?

"How are the twins?"

"Cute."

"Mmm." He stopped talking and concentrated on his ice cream. When he finished, he shoved the dish away and leaned back in his chair. "We have to figure out how we can see each other more often. This is just too hard."

"I know, but I'm not going to sneak out at night like I used to."

"Of course not. I wouldn't expect you to. Have your parents softened at all about me?"

"We don't talk much about you. In fact, not at all, anymore."

He reached across the table and held his hand palm up, seeking hers. Reluctantly, she removed her hand from her lap and placed it in his. "Belinda, we can't give up. They'll have to listen to us eventually. Surely, they're not that hard-headed that—"

"Hard-headed? That's not very nice. They just don't want to lose their dochder is all. If you think that's hard-headed—"

"I guess I used the wrong word. I mean, they have to listen to your feelings. It has to matter to them that you're in love with me. They liked me until they closed themselves off—"

"They probably still like you, but not as a suitor for their dochder. You're a threat to them. To their way of life. Surely, you can understand."

"I do, really. But I also understand that the Amish can be too radical about their beliefs. After all, I'm a Mennonite now. A plain person. Doesn't that count for anything?"

"It ain't—sorry, it *isn't*—the same and you know it." Their voices were slightly raised and the people sitting across the room stopped speaking to each other and looked over. Belinda felt all eyes on her, including Sue, who was way too attractive and made her feel even more uncomfortable.

"Let's go for a walk, Belinda. We can't talk here."

"It's cold out. Where should we go?"

"I don't know. Maybe my car. We can sit and talk in there."

He helped her on with her black woolen coat and they left the shop without saying goodbye to his friend, though

Katie knew she wasn't busy with customers and was probably watching their every move. Her cell phone remained in her pocket.

Once in the car, Jeff started up the engine to warm the interior. Belinda shivered and he leaned over and tried to place his arm around her, but she stiffened at his touch.

"Why are you acting like this? I thought you'd be excited to see me again," he reproached, and she wondered herself why she said things that were deliberately calculated to hurt him. Goodness, she'd missed him so much and now this?

"I'm sorry. It's just been a bad day, I guess. I really missed you something terrible, but I hate lying to my family. Every time we talk even, I feel guilt. I hate it."

"You shouldn't feel guilty because we're in love. There is nothing wrong with what we feel toward each other. You know that."

"But sometimes when I look over at my mother, I can tell she's holding back tears. I know it's because of me. I'm causing her pain. It's awful, Jeff." Her tears began to flow and she leaned toward him, allowing him to encircle his arms around her.

He kissed the side of her cheek. "Oh, Belinda, I know it's hard on you. I'm so sorry you have to go through this. I just wish they weren't so stubborn—"

She moved back abruptly. "There you go again! Who's stubborn? Why can't you just become Amish? It's not even that difficult at this point. You'd just have to give up your stupid car!"

"Stupid? It gets me to work on time. Does that make it stupid? What's so immoral about driving a dumb car?"

"You'll never understand. That's the problem. Everything we do seems stupid to the rest of the world. That's why I never want to be a part of your old modern world. They're blind and it seems you are too!"

"Belinda, don't. We're both just stressed out. Let's take a deep breath and talk rationally about this. First of all, I'm studying about becoming Amish. You know that. Maybe someday I can, but I can't just say I want to be Amish because my girlfriend is. They wouldn't give me the time of day if that was my reason for changing. You have to remember I have a family too. They're not happy with where I am now. My father's embarrassed by my dress. He's admitted as much."

"Goodness, he'd really be upset if his daughter-in-law looked like me! Jah, long dark clothes, hair under bonnets, no make-up, what a disgrace!"

"Belinda, be fair. We are of two different worlds. You know that."

"Then maybe we shouldn't try to make it together. Maybe it's impossible!"

"Do you believe that—really?"

She put her head in her hands and her whole body shook. "I don't know anymore. When I was at Katie's wedding, I looked around at all those gut, kind people. How do I know I'll feel safe if I leave all that? Would I eventually resent you for taking me away from my life? My loved ones?"

"I have no answer for that one, Belinda. I'd hope your love for me would be enough to compensate for whatever loss you'd have."

"My parents? My schwesters? My bruder? All my friends? Jeff, I don't know anymore. I don't know anything. I just know I'm miserable all the time. How will this end?"

He withdrew and rested his elbows on the steering wheel and held his face in his hands. "I don't know. We have to pray about it."

"I do. All the time, but I don't get answers."

"Maybe we should step back for a couple weeks and try to gain some perspective."

"Is that what you want?" She feared his answer.

"It's not what I want, but it would probably be wise. There are so many aspects to consider. We have to be intelligent about it."

"It sounds like you don't care that much anymore." Belinda's words nearly choked her.

"You know that's not true. I love you and I want to marry you, more than anything else in this world, but…"

"Jah, but?"

"I…we have to stop going by our emotions and use our heads, Belinda."

"Which means?"

"I don't know. I really don't know anymore. I wish I could just say I'd become Amish. It seems so simple, yet for some reason—lots of reasons—I can't do that at this point. Please give me time to get through this."

"You can have all the time you need," she said with a touch of sarcasm.

"Meaning?"

"Just that I'm as confused as you are, and maybe it's me who needs more time."

"Then let's give ourselves one month. Maybe things will be clear if we give it that long."

"Then what? How will we meet?"

"I'll get word to you through Carrie."

Her voice trembled. "No phone calls?"

"Honey, honey. Don't make this any harder."

"It can't be harder." She burst into fresh tears and when she looked over, he was wiping his own eyes.

"If we talk, it will be too strained. I think it best if we try to get through this without communicating. It's going to be difficult, but we need to be sure we're doing the right thing. Marriage is the most important step in a person's life, next to finding God." He touched her lips with his finger. "It means we won't be together Christmas at all."

She nodded. "It would be hard to see each other anyway. The family has so many plans during that time. We have to get around to see everyone. It's so special."

"I'm sure."

"I want to go now, Jeff. This is too hard."

"I know. I'll walk you to your buggy."

"Nee. I want to go alone. My heart is breaking."

"Oh, Belinda, maybe we should—"

"Nee. It has to be this way. If Gott is in this, it will all work out."

"I know you're right, darling."

She reached for the door handle and without turning her head, she left the warm vehicle and headed for her black buggy. She shivered as her horse began the trek back. The bitter chill reached into her very bones, adding to the depth of her despair. Love was never meant to be this painful. Her heart cried out to God, but she heard nothing in return.

Chapter Seven
Lancaster County, Pennsylvania

It had been nearly three weeks since the wedding. Christmas was over and life had returned to normal for the community.

January was dreary as the gray days loomed heavily over the entire area. Fortunately, with a new baby, Ruth was too busy to notice. Daniel brought joy to his parents as well as extra responsibilities, leaving little time to observe the weather.

Late one afternoon, Ruth laid her infant in a bassinette tucked in the corner of her kitchen, away from drafts. Then she prepared supper for her husband and son. Nathanael sat on the floor near the coal stove turning pages of a cloth book and babbling happily to himself. His interest in his new brother had waned from the first day, which had not been that impressive even then. He accepted the new member of the family and was only interested when Daniel cried loudly, which fortunately wasn't often. Ruth patted his head as she went to stir the venison and vegetable soup she'd made earlier. Noodles lay on the side ready to be inserted just before it was time to eat.

Jeremiah came through the back door and hung his woolen jacket on the peg near the door. "It's getting colder out there. Looks like snow's headed our way. I'm going to get more split wood on the porch after we eat. Can't take chances." He washed up and smiled at Nathanael who grinned at his father and tossed the book aside as he reached up to be held. Jeremiah swooped him up and took him over to see his brother, who was squirming, but bordering on sleep.

Ruth placed a tossed salad on the table and took out a loaf of fresh crusty bread from the oven, placing it on a breadboard to be cut. "Hannah came by earlier while you were in the barn, Jeremiah. She offered to watch the children for me when I take a turn helping with Oma. We've decided that Katie needs to move from the dawdi haus to her home now that she's married. It's just not right that she's had to take on so much of the care, especially with her leukemia."

"I thought that was under control."

"Jah, that's what they say, but still, she needs to be alone with Josiah."

"Can you leave the boppli for that long?"

"Nee, not while I'm nursing. I could probably keep Daniel with me, but Nathanael is a handful right now. He gets into everything."

"If Hannah's agreeable, it's fine with me. When the boppli's a little older, I can take care of him myself."

"I don't think it will be too long before Oma's fairly independent. Mamm said she's walking more now. With a walker, of course, but they're trying to wean her away from the wheelchair."

"She does seem to be making progress. Her spirits seem better, too."

"Jah, seeing her new great-grandson helps."

"And being there for Katie's wedding."

"Jah, she feels there's more to live for."

"She could live here with us, if you want."

"That's sweet, but I think she needs to be near Mamm. With the dawdi haus connected to the house, it shouldn't be long before she can move in there."

"I know your *mudder* feels more comfortable having her close. She told me herself."

Daniel let out a howl and Nathanael pulled away from his father to run to his side. He patted his brother's head as his father came over to pick the baby up.

"I need to change him and then feed him, Jeremiah. Can you keep your older sohn busy for a couple minutes?"

"Better than that—I'll get him ready for bed. Come on Nathanael, let's go change into your jammies."

Though he couldn't say more than four or five words, Nathanael understood his father. Jeremiah transferred the crying baby into Ruth's arms and followed his son up the stairs.

Ruth watched them go hand-in-hand up the stairs and she smiled. Her son was the spitting image of her dear husband. She looked down at her new one, who was sucking his fist. He, too, looked like his daed. Her heart swelled with love as she laid him on the couch to change his diaper before feeding him. Jah, maybe the next one would be a girl. How fun that would be.

The next day, as planned, Ruth and Emma rode over to their parents' home, first dropping off the little ones at their sister-in-law's house.

Hannah insisted Ruth leave Daniel as well, and since he had just been fed, Ruth took the opportunity to have an hour to herself.

Hannah never became frazzled, no matter how many little ones she had under her care. She loved children and they adored her in return. She was expecting her fifth child and as excited as with her first.

Katie was washing dishes when they arrived, while Mary and Oma worked on a new quilt. This time it was for a child, most likely for Daniel, though Oma wouldn't say. Katie looked up in surprise. "What's the occasion and where are your boppli?" she asked them.

"We are here to talk about you, Katie."

"Me? What's wrong?"

Ruth hung her jacket up and reached for her sister's. "Where's Mamm?"

"With Oma. They're quilting."

"Well let's go in so we can all be together."

"Do you want me to call the guys?"

"Nee. It doesn't concern them much," Emma said.

Once they were all seated on the bed and side chairs, Mary looked quizzically at her girls. "What's going on?"

Ruth started. "We think it's time for Katie to move into her house with her new husband. Between us and Hannah and Fannie, we can help you manage things here."

Katie's mouth dropped open and she felt tears form behind her lids. An answer to her prayers.

Oma grinned and clapped her hands. "Gut! Gut for you. Jah, I'm ever so much stronger. It won't be long, I'll be cooking my own meals. I can move into the dawdi haus."

"Mamm," Mary said, her voice choking slightly, "you're jumping way ahead of yourself. You still use the wheelchair on occasion."

"I won't anymore. I want my Katie to live in her own home. You have no idea how upset I've been, knowing I was the reason for her to remain here. That's no way to start a marriage—taking care of an old lady."

Katie raised her arm to stop Oma's words. "You know it's been no problem, Oma. I love taking care of you. Actually, if truth be told, I was nervous about having my own place right away. It's taken time to get my strength back and my self-confidence as well."

"But now, Katie? Now do you feel like you're ready?" Mary asked.

"Only if you can manage without me. I won't leave you if you have any doubts."

"Now that I'm feeling okay again and Mamm's getting more independent, I don't see any reason for you to remain here, Katie."

"And don't forget, we'll be available to help out," Emma reminded her.

"Danki. You girls are so busy with your little ones, hopefully, we can manage just fine without putting you out."

"Still, you'll need a break," Emma said.

"Jah, maybe. We shall see. Your daed and brudder aren't helpless neither."

Katie laughed. "Sometimes they pretend, I think, just to get out of things."

"Not Josiah," Oma said. "Now there's a young man who knows who he is and ain't fearful of looking silly when he helps you in the house, Katie. I bet he'll even change diapers."

The women laughed and Mary rose to put the coffee pot on. "As long as everyone's here, I'll heat up the sticky buns from yesterday and we'll have coffee together." Ruth followed her mother into the kitchen to help.

"Goodness, it seems strange not to have Nathanael and Daniel on my lap," Ruthie said as she set out cups and saucers.

Mary nodded as she measured the grinds. "Sometimes it's gut to get away, even if it's only an hour or two. You look real fine, Ruthie. Lost all your extra weight already."

"My boys keep me running."

"It's nice of you girls to suggest Katie move. I kind of forgot since we just go day to day. Of course she should be in her own place now. Josiah's worked so hard to make it special for her."

"Why don't we go over and spiff everything up before they move over, Mamm. Emma can stay back. We can make sure there are no cobwebs hiding in corners. Maybe we can even fill their larder with goodies. What do you think?"

"I like the idea. We can go today and they can move over the week-end. I just hope Katie is up to it."

Ruth stopped and laid her hands on her mother's shoulders. "We must keep praying for her, Mamm. Right now, things look gut. The doctor seems real encouraged from what Katie said."

"Jah, our family's been blessed in so many ways. We've had our trials, but the gut Lord has seen us through every single one."

Ruth nodded in agreement as she moved back to the table to lay napkins around. She whispered a prayer of thanks as she thought about her own life and how she was fulfilled. Her decision to remain Amish had been the right one and she'd never had regrets.

Chapter Eight
Holmes County, Ohio

Belinda marked her calendar with a black marking pen. It had been twenty-three days since she'd seen Jeff. Or heard from him. The longest twenty-three days of her life. Her cell phone sat under clothing in her sock drawer. It was dead anyway, just like her heart. At this point, she figured she'd never hear again. Perhaps it was just as well. The pain was nearly as intense as the day she met him at the ice cream parlor. Her parents asked her about her melancholy, but she couldn't discuss it with them or anyone else. Her friend, Rebecca, was visiting an aunt in Sarasota, Florida, so she didn't even have her to talk to. Nellie was out of the question, though sometimes she probed Belinda with questions. She definitely wouldn't understand and she might repeat everything to their parents.

At least her mother didn't try to convince her to help at the market with them. She was probably relieved that Belinda wouldn't be talking with Carrie, though she rarely showed up at her family's stand now that she attended college.

Belinda had applied for the baby-sitting job. Her parents didn't discourage her from wanting to work outside the house. Perhaps the whole family was sick of being around her at this point. She certainly wasn't very entertaining with her long face and indifferent attitude.

Belinda was pleased when the woman, Mrs. Fortina, stopped by to inform her she could have the job if she still wanted it. It would pay enough to put some money aside for her future—whatever that would hold. The hours were from eight until four, when Mrs. Fortina's stepdaughter returned home from school. She told Belinda she was sixteen and could handle the childcare until the parents returned home from work. Belinda was scheduled to begin her job the following Monday morning. Though she was nervous about it, she was anxious to get out of the house and away from the boredom she experienced during these long winter days. Her mother expected her to work on quilting, which was not something she enjoyed. The highlight of her week was Sunday when she attended services or visited family on the off-weeks.

When Monday arrived, the weather was mild enough for her to walk the half mile to the Fortina's. The stepdaughter answered the door and nodded for her to come in. "Deb's upstairs. I have to get the bus. See you later."

Belinda stood in the vestibule, wondering what she should do next. She could hear voices upstairs and assumed it was Mrs. Fortina and her husband. Did they hear the doorbell? Did they know she'd arrived?

"I'm here, Mrs. Fortina," Belinda called up after a few unsettling moments.

The woman came over to the stairwell and told her to come up. She introduced her to her husband, an attractive man in his forties. He smiled over and extended his hand. After shaking it, she was led into an over-sized nursery. The baby was in the crib sound asleep.

Mr. Fortina called back as he headed down the stairs. "We're going to be late, Deb. I'll get the car warmed up, but you'd better hurry. I'm sure Belinda can find what she needs."

"Oh, dear, I didn't realize how late it was. We have to run. I left instructions by the phone down in the hallway. My number at work is on the top, so you can call me if you have any questions. I'll be in court this afternoon, so you won't be able to reach me after one. Help yourself to lunch. Whatever you find is okay."

Belinda stood watching as Deb scurried down the hallway toward the stairs. Goodness, how nerve-wracking. Always in a hurry, just like the other Englishers she'd met. At market, people were always rushing around like someone was chasing them. Ach, not the way she lived.

The baby continued to sleep peacefully, so Belinda went down to check the directions she'd been left. The baby's schedule was all written down as well as a few minor chores for her to attend to when she had the time. Nothing too difficult.

Belinda walked through the downstairs rooms. It was huge. She figured you could call it a mansion, since it was even larger and more elegant than Carrie and Jeff's home, and she thought that was beautiful! There was a grand piano at the end of the living room and matching rose-colored sofas facing each other on each side of a heavily sculpted mantel above a fireplace. A gilded mirror hung over a long library table at the other end of the room. An enormous silk floral arrangement was centered on the table. Belinda nearly tiptoed into the next room, which was a large dining room. The highly polished table looked like mahogany and there were ten chairs placed evenly around it. Belinda had never seen such beautiful chairs with carved backs and plush cushioned seats. Did they ever really eat in such a room?

As she headed toward the back of the house the sound of dishes clanking alarmed her. Someone had sneaked in and was robbing her employers, she was sure. Her eyes darted about, looking for a means of protection. The baby! That was her first concern. The intruder would surely hear her if she tried to call the police! Nee, she'd run up and grab the baby and run out the front door to safety and then—

Goodness! A round, cheerful face appeared around the corner of the kitchen door. Certainly didn't look like a criminal. "So there you are," the stranger said calmly. "Ms. Fortina told me you'd be here."

Belinda's heart began to return to normal. The woman with curly gray hair and dancing eyes certainly looked harmless enough.

"Who are you?" she managed to get out.

"Vera Strong, honey. I'm the cook and housekeeper." She wiped her hands on her apron and reached across to shake Belinda's hand.

"Nice to meet you, Mrs. Strong."

"Just call me Vera. And you're Belinda, right?"

"Jah. That's me."

"She didn't tell me you were Amish. Are you married?"

"Nee, not yet. Maybe never," she added softly.

"Mercy, you'll be married. Look at you. Strong, healthy and pretty, to boot. I bet you have a dozen young men clambering for your hand."

"Nee. Maybe none."

"Where's that new baby? My, she's a cutie, ain't she?"

"She was sound asleep. I haven't picked her up yet. I don't even know her name."

"It's Charlotte after the mister's mother. We call her Lottie." With this a piercing cry came from a box on the wall only inches from Belinda's ear. She jumped three inches off the floor and grabbed her kapp ribbon.

Vera laughed and patted Belinda on the arm. "It's just the intercom, honey. Nothing to fret about, but your charge is calling for you. I'll put the bottle on to warm."

Once Belinda caught her breath, she headed up the stairs, two at a time, and practically ran into the nursery. She lifted the crying infant and held her against her bosom, stroked her back and uttered soothing words into her ear. Soon the baby stopped crying and settled down. A long changing table with shelves for diapers and supplies was next to the crib. After fresh diapers were applied, Belinda swaddled Lottie in a clean cotton blanket and went downstairs to the kitchen. She sat in a chair by the window to feed her while Vera filled her in on some of the details of the family.

It was Deb's first marriage and she was only twenty-nine. Her husband had been divorced for several years and had taught a class at the law school where Deb went in Philadelphia. After marrying, they moved to Ohio and joined a prestigious law practice. Vera thought it was owned by a relative, but she wasn't sure. Anyway, they'd only lived in this house for about a year and Deb got pregnant almost immediately. Vera mentioned they were good to her and gave her time off if she needed it.

"I don't think Deb was excited about having a baby right off, but she seems happier now that she's going back to work."

"Lottie is adorable. I'd hate to have to leave her if she were mine."

"I'd feel the same, but you know some women just would rather have their careers."

"What about Madison? Is she his only child?"

"He has two sons, too. They're both older and one's married and living in California. I think the other one is in graduate school in New York. I kind of forget. I never met the sons."

"So Deb's husband is a lot older?"

"He's almost fifty, but he looks good for his age."

"Jah, he's handsome. I like his gray hair."

"I don't think it will stay gray. I heard them talk about it and she wants him to dye it so he'll look younger."

"Mmm." Now it was bordering on gossip, something Belinda disapproved of, so she didn't encourage Vera to continue on that vein. "I hope they'll be pleased with me. It's a little scary. I've never done this before."

"Never taken care of a baby?"

Belinda grinned. "Oh, I've done lots of baby-sitting. No, I mean, worked away from my family."

"You'll be just fine. She won't pay much attention as long as the baby is clean and fed, that's all she cares about."

"When the daughter comes home, does she do a gut job sitting?"

"We shall see. This will be the first day. Actually, I've never seen her even hold Lottie. She pretty much just ignores her. You know teens. Well, maybe you don't know teens like her. Pretty self-centered, if you ask me."

Belinda noted the baby had fallen asleep. Only half the formula was gone, so she tickled her chin and shifted the infant to her other side to wake her up. After a few more weak sucks, Lottie turned her head and went back to sleep.

Vera looked over. "She won't take no more. I try to feed her sometimes and she's a stubborn one."

"Is she gaining okay?"

"I guess so. Her little cheeks are puffing up a little. Ain't she adorable?"

Belinda smiled at the precious child. "Oh, jah, that she is."

"I bet you'll have a dozen before you turn thirty."

"It would help to get married," Belinda said with a smile. She rose and headed for the hallway. "I may as well put her down in her crib since she's sound asleep anyway."

"When you have time, come down and we'll have tea together. I just have to finish cleaning up here and vacuum the first floor."

"Jah, that sounds gut. By the way, is it okay to use their phone for local calls?"

"You can, but keep your calls brief. And no long distance, of course. They're pretty nice people. He's nicer than she is."

Belinda started ascending the stairs. "I'll be down later."

After placing the baby safely in her crib, Belinda read over the instructions again, which she had brought upstairs with her. Nothing too difficult. It looked like she'd have a lot of time to herself. She'd have to bring a book with her tomorrow, though she'd noticed a huge bookcase when she passed by their library and it was filled with every kind of reading matter. She'd ask if she was allowed to borrow a book, but not yet. She'd go slowly at first.

The day dragged, but finally around four, Madison arrived home from school. She went directly to her room and closed the door behind her. It was half an hour before she emerged and she totally ignored Belinda, who was waiting patiently for permission to leave. Finally, Belinda could stand it no longer.

"Madison, your mother said you'd take over Lottie's care when you got home. Are you ready yet?"

"First off, Deb's not my mother and secondly, she never even gave me a chance to say no to this whole baby-sitting deal. I haven't the foggiest idea how to take care of a kid. Especially a tiny baby."

"You mean you're not going to take over her care now?" Belinda could hardly believe what she was hearing.

"I'll stay in my room in case she cries, but I have homework. Besides, my friend's coming by soon. Vera can take care of the kid."

Belinda stared at the girl. How selfish! Then she went upstairs, picked up Lottie and wrapped the blanket snuggly around her delicate body for warmth. She carried her downstairs into the kitchen where Vera was preparing dinner. She looked over at Belinda, her brows raised.

"I don't know what to do. I'm supposed to leave Lottie in Madison's care, but she's made it obvious that she has no intention of really caring for the child. I can't just walk out knowing that. And you're busy getting supper ready. Goodness, what should I do?"

"That little tart. She does absolutely nothing around here. She should go live with her mother. Let me finish up my prep work and I'll take over. I'll get her car seat out of the hall closet and set her in that. Poor little thing. It seems no one really cares about her."

"I can stay till they get home. I don't want you to have to do everything."

"Honey, sometimes it's eight o'clock before they get home. No, you go along now. It's getting dark and you walked over, didn't you?"

"Well, if you think it's okay."

"I do. Go now. I'll see you tomorrow morning."

"If you're sure, okay."

"Hey, I live here and I have no family, so it's not a problem for me. Besides, I love little Lottie. She's like my grandchild."

"Danki. I'll go then."

When she arrived home, Belinda was met at the door by Nellie. "You just missed her."

"Who?"

"Carrie. She came by to see you."

"Oh, no. What did she say?" Belinda's heart raced.

"Not much. She apologized for not stopping by sooner. She was sick or something."

"She was alone?"

"Jah. She left you a letter."

Belinda glanced at her sister's hand and noted a small envelope.

"Here. I didn't tell Mamm about the note."

"Danki, Nell. I appreciate that. No sense causing a scene."

"That's what I figured. Mamm's at the neighbors."

"I'm going up to my room for a few minutes and then I'll be down to help with supper. Smells gut in here."

"Jah, chicken and dumplings."

Belinda went up to her room and opened the note. Her hands shook as she noted Jeff's writing. Was it good-bye forever?

Chapter Nine
Lancaster County, Pennsylvania

The men in the family helped Katie and Josiah move in over the week-end. Mary parted with an old dresser and two straight back chairs to help furnish one of the guest rooms. Mark, one of Katie's older brothers and his wife, Hannah, had extra towels to contribute and her other older brother, Abram and his wife Fannie, had a family desk they no longer needed. Katie was thrilled to receive the desk, which was solid pine with a flat top and three drawers on each side. If she went back to teaching, she could use it for her extra supplies and workbooks.

The women arrived around four and brought enough food for a week. Even Oma came. It was the first time she'd been through the house and though she didn't make it up the stairs she raved about the job Josiah had done on the first floor—especially in the kitchen. "You have a lot of gut skills, young man. It looks very nice in here. My Katie should be happy living in such luxury."

Josiah grinned at the compliment and nodded. "My Katie-girl would be happy anywhere. She's ever so pleasant."

Mary overheard them and nodded in agreement. "She had her moments, Josiah, believe me, but you've made her a happy woman."

Katie walked in from the living room, where she had told her brothers where to set the desk. She went over to Josiah and took his hand. "You excited?"

"Oh, jah. A little. How 'bout you?"

She nodded and smiled at him. "We won't have to worry about food for awhile."

After they ate and everyone had perused the whole house and admired the skills of Josiah, the crowd began to disperse. Katie and Josiah sat down to discuss the day. It was already after eight.

"Katie, I'm concerned about one thing, which I haven't mentioned."

She looked over at him and nodded. "Jah?"

"It's about having boppli."

Her heart dropped. Was he already upset with her?

"What about it?"

"Do you think we should be careful not to get you in a family way? I mean, with your illness and all, it would be better if you didn't…you know. You told me you'd have to stop the medication."

"I think we should leave it in the Lord's hands."

"I just don't want anything to happen to you, honey." He sat closer to her on the sofa and put his arm around her shoulders.

Katie settled into his embrace. "I think if I do become in a family way, that we can trust everything will be fine."

"Do you think you should talk to the doctor again?"

"I don't know. Maybe. I just want to go about our marriage without worrying one way or the other about it."

"I'd like to say I can do the same, but I'd be lying. I do worry about it. We can adopt a child you know."

"It's not that easy, besides…" Katie felt her eyes fill up.

"Honey, don't. We don't have to talk about it now. We'll just take it a day at a time. Okay?"

She nodded and took a tissue from her pocket and blew her nose. "I just want to enjoy every moment with my husband in our new home."

"Then that's what we'll do. Now kiss your husband and then we should get you to bed. It's been a long day."

"You can say that again. I am tired tonight, but happy."
She blinked back any further tears and leaned against him
as he met her lips with his. Then they went up to spend
their first night together in their new home. God had
answered so many of her prayers. Surely, he'd answer one
more.

Holmes County, Ohio

Belinda sat on her bed as she prepared herself to read
Jeff's note. Her heart pounded as she began the letter.

Dear Belinda,
It seems like forever since we were together.
Perhaps having the separation was the wrong thing to
do. I don't know. All I know is that I still love you and
hope you'll one day marry me. If you have discovered
over the past days that you no longer feel the same, I
will try to understand. I know this is a difficult time for
you as well.
It's frustrating not to be able to talk to you. I gave
in and tried to call you, but I guess you don't use your
phone anymore. Fortunately, the last weeks have been
very busy for me. I've worked lots of extra hours and
now classes have started again and the new courses are
difficult and require a lot of study time, which is okay
since I don't see you now and it helps pass the time a
little.
I believe we can work everything out in the end. I
hope you feel the same. It will mean compromise on
each of our parts, but things can work for us to be
together again. Please call me somehow—soon.
If I don't hear, I will assume you are calling it off, but I
think you owe it to me to see me in person no matter
what you've decided. Of course, I'm praying (literally)

that you still care as much as you did. I'm trying to
prepare myself for whatever you've decided.
                  Love forever,   Jeff

The last few words blurred as tears filled her eyes. He still cared. Thank God, but there was nothing in there to make her think he was going to go Amish. In fact, just the opposite, since he mentioned compromise. Originally she had believed in her heart that she could go the way of the Mennonites, but now, even that seemed too much to ask of her. Her family would be so devastated if she left. Even though she might not actually be banned, she would no longer be accepted by her Plain people in the community.

He's the one who needed to compromise more. After all, now that he was already a Mennonite, he could jump over to Amish with ease, for heaven's sake. His family wouldn't ban him!

But forgetting all that, he signed it 'love forever' which was a long time. She smiled through her tears as she pictured him. He was everything she ever wanted in a mate. Tomorrow when she was at work, she'd place a call to him and they would make plans to see each other. They'd struggled through these last weeks trying to do the right thing and it had been pure torture. It wasn't fair to expect people in love like this to turn from each other. Nee, it wasn't fair at all. Love should win out.

Belinda tucked the letter inside her apron pocket along with the cell phone. Tomorrow they would both go with her and tomorrow she'd hear his voice once again. Sleep would not come easily tonight.

Chapter Ten
Holmes County, Ohio

The sun finally peeked out from the clouds as Belinda made her way to the Fortina's house. Her steps were quick as she hummed a familiar song from the Singings. Happy. Yes, she was happy for the first time in so many days. Even her mother noticed it before she left the house and commented on the change. "I guess you like sitting for boppli," she'd added.

"Maybe so," Belinda had said, not sharing her true reasons for her change in demeanor.

When she approached the house, Madison came through the front door, carrying a load of books. She barely acknowledged Belinda, but she left the door open for her.

"See you later, Madison," Belinda called out after her.

"Yeah. Suppose so." A friend was waiting at the end of the drive and he waved to Madison as she stepped up her pace.

Belinda entered the home and closed the door behind her. She could hear voices coming from upstairs and the baby's cries. It was awkward. Should she go right up?

"I'm here, Mrs. Fortina," she called up by the foot of the stairs.

The woman appeared, looking frazzled. "There you are. Don't you hear Charlotte? She's been screaming for an hour. Please get her for me. I'm running late."

Belinda went up quickly and entered the nursery where Lottie had kicked off her blankets and was crying so hard, her little face was beet-red. When she lifted her she could tell she needed changing by the odor. "Poor boppli, don't cry. I'll have you all cleaned up in a minute." But first she held her close and patted her back. "Settle down, little one. Shhhh." Almost instantly, Lottie stopped sobbing, though her little body trembled from her recent tears. "Now, now. We'll get you something to drink, don't you worry."

Mr. Fortina looked in at them as he headed toward the stairs. "I'm glad you got her quieted down. She spent half the night screaming. I hope she's not sick. Call us if she runs a fever."

"I will. She doesn't feel hot, but maybe she has a tummy ache. I'll hold her for a while. Please don't worry."

He smiled broadly. "No, I think she's in good hands. We'll see you later."

After they left and the baby was changed into a fresh diaper and a clean cotton nightie, Belinda took her down to the kitchen where a warm bottle sat waiting in a pan of hot water. Vera was wiping down the counters when she came in.

"Well look at my Lottie. You sure had a rough morning, young lady," she said as she patted the baby's arm.

"I see you have her bottle ready. *Danki,* I mean thanks," Belinda said.

"Danki is cute. Just say it when you want. I know some Pennsylvania Dutch."

"Thanks," she said in return and then giggled. "I mean, danki."

Belinda reached for the bottle with her free hand and wiped the water off the bottom on a dishtowel, which laid next to it. Then she sat down on a kitchen chair and placed the bottle to Lottie's mouth. She pushed the nipple out with her tongue and turned her head.

"You must be hungry, sweetheart. Come on." Belinda inserted the nipple again but received the same response.

"I think the child's too tired to care about food. I've heard her cry half the night. Maybe after she sleeps a little, you should try again."

"Jah, I guess so. I just hope she's not sick. Mr. Fortina seemed concerned."

"Glad someone is," Vera said, brows furrowed.

"I guess I'll lay her in her crib if she's going to sleep anyway."

"I think she needs to be held more than she needs sleep."

"Jah? Maybe so. Then I'll just stay here with you and keep her cozy in my arms. Dear sweet boppli. Such a gift from Gott."

Vera grinned over. "I'm glad they found you. That's a blessing from God right there, if you ask me."

Vera went into her own apartment and came back carrying a small rocker for Belinda to use. She set it by the bay window and turned on the radio. After finding a music station, which played soft 'elevator' music, she turned it down low. "There, that should help," she said as Belinda settled into the rocker with Lottie. After more than an hour, the baby awoke and before she could cry, Vera had a fresh bottle of formula ready. This time Lottie pulled at the nipple with gusto and got down four whole ounces. A new record, according to Vera.

Afterwards, Belinda burped her, then took her upstairs to change her diaper. Lottie fell asleep almost immediately, so Belinda laid her down for a real nap. This would be a perfect time to call Jeff. She could use the house phone. At the same time, she'd re-charge her battery in the nursery. Belinda felt uneasy as she plugged it in. Should she have asked permission first? It seemed like a small thing, but it still bothered her. She went downstairs, and mentioned to Vera that she was making a local call before she dialed Jeff's number. Moistening her lips in preparation for his voice, she waited while the ringing continued. The answering machine picked up and then she left a short message, giving him the Fortina's phone number. It felt awkward to be talking to a machine after so many days apart. Seemed so unnatural. She realized she should have given him a deadline for calling back, since she'd be leaving around four. Hopefully, she'd hear back before then.

Lottie slept for three whole hours and when she awoke, Belinda went through the change, bottle, and change routine once again. She enjoyed holding the baby and extended the time so she could bond with the child. Oh, how wonderful-gut it would be to one day have her own boppli.

Around three, Vera answered the house phone and called up to Belinda, who was folding baby clothes from the dryer. Belinda took the call in the upstairs hall and was relieved to hear Jeff's voice on the other end. At first it was awkward, but before five minutes passed, he had her smiling into the phone. "Jah, I've missed hearing your voice, too. You know that." Then she explained about her new job.

"That's great! Now you can re-charge your phone every time you work there," he said.

"Yah, that will work gut. I don't feel right staying on their phone too long, though."

"I understand, but we can make our plans now and next time you can use your own phone. I have to see you soon. It's driving me crazy to be apart from you."

Belinda nodded without thinking. "Me, too."

"So when do you get off today?"

"I'm supposed to be off at four, but it's not that easy in reality."

"You can call me when you do get done there and I'll come by and pick you up. You said you walked there, right?"

"Jah, but my parents expect me home by five."

"We'll have a few minutes anyway."

"That's better than nothing. Okay, I'll wait at the end of the drive here." She gave him the address. Then she hung up and went in to finish the clothes. It was difficult to concentrate on anything now that she knew she'd see Jeff. Oh, that all would go well.

At four, the bus stopped out front and Madison came in, this time with a male friend. She didn't bother to introduce anyone and led him upstairs into her room, shutting the door behind her. Belinda, shocked at her rudeness and the fact she was entertaining a young man in her bedroom, carried Lottie down to the living room where Vera was polishing furniture.

She looked up as Belinda came in. "You look as mad as a two-headed kangaroo," Vera said, holding back a grin.

"It's Madison! I can't believe that girl!" Belinda told Vera what happened.

"That's not unusual. She entertains a lot."

"Do her parents know?"

"I tried to talk to Deb about it, but she didn't want to hear it. She just frowned and told me to mind my own business. So I do."

"They should know the girl isn't holding up her end of this baby-sitting arrangement. I really can't stay much longer."

"I'll take Lottie so you can leave. Just let me put this polish away and scrub my hands. She should be ready for a feeding soon."

Belinda followed her into the kitchen and waited as she cleaned up. After she transferred the baby, she unplugged her phone and headed out the door, calling Jeff as she walked toward the street.

Ten minutes later, he pulled up in his car. Her heart sang as he reached across the seat to open her side of the car. She climbed in and he drove a few yards to a wide section of berm, where he pulled over and stopped the car. Then he reached across the seat and pulled Belinda closer to him. Before she realized it, he had his lips on hers and she responded to him. The scent of his familiar after-shave reached her senses and she kept her cheek next to his, relishing the moment.

"These have been the longest days of my life," he said softly, as he moved back slightly and looked into her eyes.

"For me, too. I was afraid you'd changed your mind and I might never hear from you again."

"Oh, Belinda, how could you even think that? You know how much I love you."

"Things are so difficult between us, though. Sometimes I just want to run away with you and forget everyone and everything else in the world."

"I know, but we can't do that. You know it would be wrong."

"Jah. It just goes through my head once in a while, but I know it's impossible."

"So tell me about your job?"

She filled him in on the Fortina family and described her day."

"Good practice," he said as he continued to hold her hand in his.

"What about you, Jeff? Carrie said you were super busy."

"I try to be, to tell you the truth. I put as many hours in on the job as I can, but now that Christmas is over, business at the shop has slowed down a lot. He still uses me, but his wife helps out, too. I guess there isn't that much money coming in to pay me for as many hours. I've saved a lot though. Over two thousand dollars."

"Wow! That's wonderful-gut. I hope to save from this job, too, but it doesn't pay that much to begin with."

"At least it helps you to be out of the house, doesn't it?"

"It does, though it's an easy job and I don't have too much to do when Lottie sleeps."

"As she gets older, she'll be awake more."

"Jah, that's true. I better be glad for this time."

"We have to make plans. We have to see each other at least once a week, Belinda."

"I agree. Even though I hate—"

"I know, I know. Me too. It's not easy to sneak around like this, but there's no other way right now. We'll figure something out. Do you get off earlier any other day of the week? I know week-ends would be hard for you to get away."

"Jah. Almost impossible. I get off the same time each day during the week."

"Mmm. Maybe you could tell a little white lie to your family and say you have to work late once a week."

"Oh, Jeff, I hate to lie again."

"How else can we see each other then? Don't you care?"

Belinda's throat tightened. His eyes looked so pained. "Of course I do. Okay, I'll tell them I'll be home closer to six. That will give us a little more time together."

"How about seven?"

"Nee, they might check."

"Alright, six it is. Mondays?"

"I guess."

"Belinda, don't you think it's worth a small lie to see me? You know I don't like it any better than you do, but your parents don't leave us much choice."

A long sigh came from her lips. "You're right, I guess. I'd better walk the rest of the way now so no one sees your car."

"Not yet. It's only quarter of five. Give me a few more minutes. It has to last a whole week. Come let me kiss you."

She moved closer to him and allowed him to engage her again in a long, tender kiss. She felt a tear trickle down her cheek as it reached her lips. He pulled back slightly. "Sweetheart, don't cry. It won't always be like this. I promise."

"It would be so simple if you were Amish."

"Shhh. No more talking." He wiped her tears with his hand and gently kissed her cheeks. "I'll take you nearer to your home. It will save time."

She moved away and wrapped her jacket closer to her shivering body. Even though the car was warm, she felt cold inside. After he let her out he pulled away and she went quickly to the house where her mother was looking out the window for her. When she came in, Grace asked her about her day and why she was late.

"It's hard to leave right away, Mamm. The dochder needs time to change and all. In fact Monday's I'll have to stay until six from now on."

"I thought you said the housekeeper helped out when she was needed."

"Well, sometimes, but they want me to stay later. How can I say no?"

"I guess. They should pay you more for your time."

"It's okay. I don't mind. What's for supper?" Time to change the subject.

"Meatloaf and mashed potatoes tonight and we'll need a jar of beans from the basement."

"I'll get them after I hang my coat up." Why was her hand shaking? Goodness, it was so easy to lie before. Was God expecting better of her now? It wouldn't be forever. Hopefully, God would understand.

Chapter Eleven
Holmes County, Ohio

Three weeks had past since Belinda and Jeff started seeing each other again. Though the time was short to be together, they spoke on the phone each night and that helped with the loneliness. Sunday they didn't try to speak since the families spent time together and it was too difficult to find an opportunity.

Jeff enjoyed the services at the Meetinghouse. He usually sat with his new friends in the back of the room and afterward they often went out for breakfast or lunch together. Their group of eight—all singles—planned get-togethers on Saturdays throughout the year. In the good weather, it was outdoor events like picnics and softball, but this time of year, they sometimes just hung out at the meetinghouse and played board games.

Jeff spent more time than ever with his Mennonite friends. His old friends pretty much ignored him now since he'd become plain. It was hurtful in a way, but he realized when he converted, it might happen. Persecution was part of the deal. Even the Bible spoke of that.

This Sunday, the group headed off to a local pizza shop and sat at two tables pushed together. Carrie came along and sat at the other end next to Randy.

As they waited for their order, Megan, a pretty petite brunette his age, who was sitting next to Jeff, asked him all about his work and school. It turned out she too was taking evening courses at the same school.

"I'm studying computer science," she informed him. "There's so much to learn, though. Sometimes it's overwhelming."

"I know what you mean," Jeff said. "Even my courses are demanding."

"What are you aiming to do when you graduate?"

"I'm not all that sure. I'd like to open my own landscaping business, but that takes a lot of cash."

"I know. Any business does, I'm afraid. I'll probably look for a job with a corporation."

"Will you stay local?"

"I want to, but if I have to move for a good position, then so be it."

The waiter showed up with their drink order and Jeff squeezed lemon into his iced tea. Megan smiled over. "Do you want my lemon, too? I don't use it."

"Sure." He grinned. "Thanks."

"Are you glad you switched to our church, Jeff?"

"Actually, I am. I really feel I'm where I belong."

"I wasn't always a Mennonite, either. I used to be Amish."

His jaw dropped. "Really? Wow!"

She laughed. "It really wasn't that big a deal to switch, although my family hasn't made it easy on me. My main reason for leaving was the education thing. For a couple years before I left, I studied in secret. They simply couldn't understand my need to accomplish something on my own. I mean, the whole marriage, baby thing is fine, but I wanted more. Can you understand?"

"I do. Believe me, I really do. I have a girlfriend and we're pretty serious, but she's Amish and she wants more than anything for me to become Amish too. That way her family will accept this whole situation, but so far I'm having trouble making that decision."

"It's not for everyone. Why doesn't she leave and become a Mennonite? We have pretty much the same morals, just less stringent rules."

"That may be the way this gets resolved. I hope so, because I've been seeing an Amish guy almost every week-end and he's teaching me about all the rules and customs. A lot of them would not be a big deal, but there are others…"

"How well I know. Some bishops actually set banns if you leave. Others are more lenient. They kind of look the other way so the families aren't forced to shun their loved ones. That's how it is with me. I still spend time at home, but honestly, Jeff, it's not the same. Your girlfriend needs to know it will affect her relationships at home no matter how strict or lenient her district bishop is."

"Where was your district?"

"Oh, it was in Indiana. I moved here last year. I'm sharing an apartment with a friend I met at a mission trip. I hope to go to Philadelphia next year when I've saved enough money. I plan to get my diploma at the university there."

"You really are determined, aren't you?" he said as he reached for his iced tea.

"Yes. And I can still have the marriage thing and all down the road. I'm in no hurry."

"So no boyfriend?"

She smiled. "Not yet. I went with a guy back home for a while, but he wasn't the one. I'll know when I meet 'Mr. Right.'"

"Make room for the pizzas," Randy called out to the group as the waiter arrived with two huge pies. Before anyone reached for a piece, Randy gave a blessing over the food. Jeff reached over and removed a piece first for Megan and then one for himself. Bob, a young man on his other side noticed.

"So where's my piece, brother?"

"Hey, I figured you were old enough to pick out your own," Jeff said with a smile.

"I guess I'm not as pretty as Megan," Bob said, causing Jeff to question his own action. Belinda would not approve of his behavior, though he was only being polite, certainly nothing more.

Lancaster County, Pennsylvania

Katie carried her laundry basket outdoors. It was early March and ten degrees above normal. She noted crocuses popping up near the porch and smiled at the brilliant colors contrasting with the dull browns and grays of the winter aftermath. Spring was her favorite season and though the tree limbs were still barren, soon new life would be visible as buds formed.

Her own life felt barren. Last night her monthly had appeared. Though she didn't speak further to Josiah about her feelings, she hoped in her heart, she would one day become pregnant with his child. Once a month was a reminder that it might never be so. She tried not to be disappointed and instead concentrate on her life as his wife, but it didn't take long to clean their small farmhouse and cook three meals a day. It left hours for reading and mending and thinking. She drew diagrams for her vegetable garden and Josiah planned to till a separate section near the barn for an herb garden.

Becky had stopped by the day before and mentioned again about teaching. Katie hadn't yet approached Josiah about the possibility of returning to the school house, but she felt so much healthier now and her visits to the oncologist were cut in half. Surely it would be all right if she put in a few hours a day teaching. It would help take her mind off her inability to be in a family way. That was for sure.

The next evening as they sat doing their devotions together, she brought up the subject of teaching.

"If that's what you want to do, Katie, that's fine with me. Are you sure you're feeling up to it? You know those kids can take a lot out of you."

"True, but Becky's the head teacher now. I'd be assisting her, is all."

"If she needs you and you're well enough, I have no objections."

"Of course, if I should become—" Her voice trailed off.

His eyes sought hers. "In a family way?"

"Jah."

"Then you could leave your teaching position, of course. I hope you're not counting on that, Katie-girl. You know it probably won't happen. You have to accept that fact."

"But if Gott—"

"I know. And if it happens, I'll be just as happy as you, but we shouldn't reckon on it. I have my ears open if someone mentions an orphan or something. You never know."

"Me, too. But it's rare in our community to hear of an unwanted baby or an orphan. With such large families, there's always someone to help raise a child who suddenly finds himself without a parent."

"It's true, Katie, but again we have to leave it in Gott's hands. He knows best."

"I may ride over to the school house later and talk to Becky about teaching. Danki, for understanding, Josiah. It's not like I'm not happy with you. Goodness gracious— I've never been happier, but I find I have a lot of time on my hands. In the summer, when school is out, I'll be home to start canning and all. It should work out."

She looked over at Josiah and he nodded.

"You seem to keep busy every single hour," she added. "Will you start tilling soon?"

"The ground's too wet to till. I'm postponing the job till things dry up somewhat. Now I'm just making plans for the early crops. It won't be long before it will be planting time."

"I know you're excited. It'll be your first full year here."

He reached over to her and placed his arm around her. "Every day is a special blessing. Let's thank the Lord together, Katie." They bowed their heads in gratitude.

Chapter Twelve
Holmes County, Ohio

Now that Lottie was three-months-old, she was feeding less frequently and now able to smile. Belinda had grown to love the sweet child and looked forward to sitting for her during the week. The family seemed preoccupied with their own activities, but between Vera and Belinda, Lottie was given the care she needed, though it concerned them that the family wasn't more involved in her well-being. As far as Lottie's half-sister was concerned, she was practically non-existent. She never participated in the child's care and Vera didn't bother to tell the parents. What would be accomplished? They appeared disinterested.

Monday afternoons were still the only opportunity for Jeff and Belinda to spend time together. Now that it was warming up, they usually parked near a creek and walked for the fresh air. Belinda's boots got muddy sometimes, but she wiped them down before returning home. It no longer bothered her that the parents thought she was working until six. After all, she rationalized, she wouldn't have to lie, if they were the least bit understanding. In a way, it was their own fault.

On this Monday as they walked hand-in-hand along a pathway to the creek, Jeff mentioned Megan, who he confided in about Belinda's situation when they were together.

"Megan? Who's that?"

He told her about the group going out after services and how he happened to end up sitting next to her. He refrained from mentioning that they nearly always found themselves seated together when they went out. He wasn't sure how it happened, but he refused to pursue the question further, even to himself.

"Why do you talk to another girl about me? I don't like that," Belinda began.

"It's nothing really. I guess 'cause I told her about you and she'd been Amish before—well, it just…"

"Just what?"

"I don't know. There's nothing going on, if that's what you're hinting at. She's merely a friend."

"Mmm." Belinda stepped up her pace and dropped his hand. She arrived at the bank of the creek just before he did.

"Don't act like this. It's stupid to be jealous of someone you don't even know. Don't you trust me?"

"Why do you ask that? Trust has nothing to do with it. I just don't like you confiding in a girl. I'm here, if you need to talk."

"Look, Belinda. You're making too much out of this. Don't you ever talk to other guys besides me?"

"Not very often. Only Zeke once in a while when he comes by to deliver a message from his sister."

"She can't deliver her own?"

"She's in Florida and she hates writing, so she only corresponds with her family once a week. Goodness, are you a little green around the edges?"

Jeff folded his arms and stared into the creek, now lively from the melted snows.

"Are you?" Belinda asked again.

"Of course not. You can talk to anyone you please."

"Do you care if I go to the Sings? Nellie's old enough to attend, but she's nervous to go by herself. I told her I'd go with her a couple times till she feels comfortable, but I wanted to talk to you about it first."

"That's not necessary. You see, I *trust* you."

"That's unfair. You know I trust you, but sometimes girls get the wrong idea. Maybe this Megan has eyes for you."

"She knows about you. She's not interested in guys. She told me herself. She's studying computer and hopes to get her degree."

"Goodness, you know a lot about her. Is she pretty?"

Jeff's mouth twitched and he looked down at his feet. "How should I know?"

"Don't you have eyes?"

"I guess some people would think she was kind of pretty."

"And you, Jeff. What do you think?" Belinda's words came out, enunciated in sharp tones.

"I don't like your line of questioning. Let's talk about something else."

"That sounds like an answer to me. So she's pretty."

"Belinda, how did you come up with that conclusion?"

"Men are so easy to read. Nee, we won't talk about it again, but you know how I feel about you talking to her, so I hope you'll consider my feelings."

"Of course. And Zeke isn't so bad looking either, besides I know he thinks of you as more than a friend."

"And how on earth do you know that?"

"Remember, I met him at your place. It was pretty obvious. The guy has a thing for you."

"That shouldn't surprise you. There have been several guys who've shown an interest. I may not have pretty clothes and flashy hair and all, but it ain't keeping the looks away! Oh, sorry, not ain't. I meant doesn't," she added.

"You're still upset with me for correcting your speech. That was ages ago. Get over it."

Belinda's mouth dropped open and she pushed him aside and headed back toward the road. "I'll walk home, thank you."

"Wait, Belinda. Don't go off in a huff. I didn't mean anything by that remark. Really."

She kept walking. Her heart pumped briskly. *That Megan can have him! He's nothing but trouble at this point.*

By the time she reached the edge of her property her anger was gone and in its place was sorrow and regret. She shouldn't have reacted the way she did. Mercy, she just was on edge all the time now. Only when she was caring for Lottie was she able to feel any peace. When was this going to end? Would there ever be a marriage between them when they couldn't even spend an hour a week together without friction. What had become of their relationship? She heard his car zoom past her and saw his rigid posture out of the corner of her eye. Would she ever hear from him again?

Lancaster County, Pennsylvania

It felt good to be teaching again. Katie sat in the back with the older children and corrected their test papers while Becky read to the younger ones. The coal stove cooked away, removing the spring chill from the one room which housed the thirty students comfortably as they studied together. The troublemakers had calmed down and between Becky and Katie's disciplinary skills, things were relatively peaceful.

After the dismissal, the children made their way home by buggy or foot as Katie wiped down the board and Becky took out her planner for the next day. When everything was done, they sat for a few minutes before heading to their homes.

"How do you like married life?" Becky asked as she passed a bag of chips to Katie, who took several and laid them on a piece of paper.

"Ever so much, Becky. I highly recommend it."

"Oh, jah, like I don't know. If that brudder of yours ever decides to settle down, I hope he remembers his schwester's best friend."

"Jah, me, too. I'm afraid he's enjoying all the female attention he gets."

"So I notice. It seems every single Amish girl in our district has a fancy for him. I don't stand a chance, that's for sure."

"Nee, not true, Beck. I think he kind of likes you the best."

Becky's eyes lit up. "Really? What makes you think that?"

"Well, it's not like he's said, it's just that when I was living at the farm, he seemed to show up at the house more when you were around. I notice those things."

"He was real nice to me when we were together by the brook when you were sick. I think he needed to talk to someone about his feelings."

"He's so sweet sometimes. Even though he never said much, I knew he really cared about me getting better. Sometimes I'd catch a look or a tone of voice. I think it's just hard for guys to express their feelings."

"You two have always been close. I'm open to other guys though, Katie. I'm not gonna wait forever for him to make up his mind."

"Any one you're interested in?"

"Not really, though a couple of the guys are kind of cute."

"Can you name names?"

"I can, but I'd rather not. Nee, I'll just wait until one of them notices me—if ever."

"You're a gut catch for someone, Becky. You know that."

"I'm not pretty like you, Katie. And I'm not real smart and all."

"Don't say that. Of course you are and you quilt really gut."

"Like the guys care about quilting."

"Be patient. The right guy will come around and I'm actually praying that the right guy will be Wayne."

"Me, too. I pray it every night. So let's head home. I m gonna make a batch of fudge tonight so you can take some home to Wayne tomorrow."

"You can deliver it yourself after school let's out. Wayne's been helping Josiah with the new windmill he's installing. You haven't been to our new place for a meal yet. Come and stay for supper. I'll make burgers and baked potatoes."

"That's a deal, Katie. Tomorrow after school though, I'll go home first and freshen up. I'm so glad you're my friend. Even without your bruder, you're the best friend ever."

The girls went out arm-in-arm to their buggies.

Chapter Thirteen
Holmes County, Ohio

"Belinda, did you hear me?" Grace's voice finally reached Belinda's consciousness.

"I'm sorry, Mamm. What did you say?"

"I asked you to pass the rolls."

Belinda reached over for the basket of wheat rolls and handed them to her mother. Nellie and Gideon glanced at each other and Nellie giggled into her napkin.

"What's so funny, little one," her daed, Jed asked.

"It's just Belinda. She's like in another world all the time. It's funny, is all."

"I am not! Okay, sometimes I'm thinking of something else and I don't pay attention."

"Like all the time. You have a droopy face on you, too," Nellie added.

"That's enough. Leave your schwester alone," Grace said. She turned to Belinda and cocked her head to the side. "You don't seem like yourself lately, though. You feel okay?"

"I'm fine."

The family continued to eat. The only sound came from silverware clicking against the plates. Silence prevailed for several minutes. Finally, Nellie announced quietly, "I know what's wrong with Belinda."

Everyone stopped eating and looked over.

"It's because of Jeff. She's sad."

Belinda burst into tears and left the table without asking permission.

Jed looked over at Grace as his mouth dropped open. "What's all this about?"

"I guess she's still grieving over Jeff," Grace said. She lifted her fork and pushed her remaining peas around her plate.

"It's been a while now. Goodness, the girl can't still be pining away," Jed said.

"Oh, jah, Daed. She can. Take my word for it," Nellie said with her brows creased.

"That's being silly. There are plenty of gut Amishmen out there, for heaven's sake."

"It takes time, Jed," Grace said as she leaned back in her chair. "I feel bad for our dochder. She's taking it hard, but she's been gut about not seeing him. At least she's obedient."

Nellie finished her supper and started to rise to clear the dishes.

Jed looked over with a scowl. "Sit, Nellie. We need to talk about Belinda. She needs us to help get her through this. First off, I don't want you to make fun of her again. That ain't nice."

Nellie sat still, looking down at her lap. "Sorry. I'll try to be nicer. It gets on my nerves sometimes, is all."

"Jah, mine too," Gideon added. "She's such a grouch."

"I'll speak to her about it later. Right now she needs time to get through her feelings," Jed said. Grace nodded.

"I thought she seemed to like Zeke the last time he was over, "Gideon said. "She certainly laughed at his jokes a lot and they weren't all that funny."

Grace smiled at her son. "Give her time. I've invited Zeke for dinner Sunday. She doesn't know yet, but I think it would be gut for them to get to know each other better."

"She's gonna be mad, Mamm. I know it." Nellie put her arms on her chest and pouted.

"She'll get over it. By the way, I thought she was going to go to a Sing with you, Nellie."

"Jah, she said she would. I'll ask her again."

"Maybe she'll meet someone there this time." Grace loosened her apron ties and stood to fill dishes of tapioca pudding she'd made earlier.

"Not now, Grace," Jed said as he watched her reach for the pudding. "I'm too full and besides, I need to check one of the cows. She was making weird noises earlier. I hope she ain't sick."

"We'll all wait then. In the meantime, I'll go check on Belinda. Nellie, redd-up the kitchen for me."

When Grace reached Belinda's bedroom, she heard her muffled cries. Her heart was troubled for her daughter. She knocked and Belinda told her to come in. Grace sat at the edge of the bed and patted Belinda's arm. "I'm sorry you're still hurting, Belinda. I know it must be hard on you to break off with someone you care about."

Belinda reached for tissues and blew her nose. Then she sat up and reached over for her mother. They held each other for several minutes before speaking. "Mamm, I need to tell you something. Please don't get too mad."

Grace pulled back and nodded. "Go ahead."

"It's just that…well…we haven't finally broken up. I mean we still talk on the phone sometimes."

"Mmm. But you don't see him behind our backs, do you?"

Belinda felt a stab in her heart. How easy it would be to continue to lie, but… "I'm sorry. We see each other once in a while."

Grace's expression showed alarm. Her brows rose and her mouth dropped open. "Belinda, how could you? You promised!"

"I know. I shouldn't have. It's just so hard on us and we still love each other. It just doesn't seem fair to make us break up over this Amish thing."

"This 'Amish thing' is not something small. It's our life—our way of living in this world. Leaving it could mean you'd be banned."

"But I haven't taken my kneeling vows. They wouldn't bann me."

"Even if you weren't actually banned, you'd never be truly accepted again by the community. You know that. You'd get involved in the Mennonite world. Do you want that? To never be a strong part of your community or family again? Is any man worth that kind of sacrifice?"

Belinda burst into fresh tears. "I don't know. I'm so miserable. I hate my life right now. Whoever thought love could bring so much pain?"

"It shouldn't. If you'd only get yourself over this young man and allow your feelings to grow for an Amishman, your life would straighten out real quick-like. You're hurting too many people, Belinda. It just ain't fair to hurt your family so much. We've never given you anything but love. Can't you see what's happening to us? To the whole family?"

Belinda shook her head, keeping her hands over her wet face. "I know it's hurting everyone. I don't mean to cause anyone pain, but we just want to get married. I don't think that's asking too much."

"Maybe it is asking too much. You need to pray about it and read the Bible. Don't forget what it says about respecting your parents. That's not my law, Belinda—it's Gott's law."

"Mamm, please don't ever shun me. Even if the Bishop says you have to, please don't do that to me. I'd never get over it." Belinda lifted her face and through blurry eyes looked into her mother's face.

Tears were streaming down her mother's cheeks now as she shook her head. "Hold me, dochder."

Belinda surrounded her mother with her arms and held her, sobbing as she did so. They remained entwined for several minutes and finally, Grace moved back. "I have to go downstairs now. Your daed will be wanting his pudding by now. You want to join us?"

Belinda shook her head. "Not yet. I'm too upset. Mamm?"

"Jah?"

"I love you."

"Oh, *liebschen*. I love you, too."

Grace rose slowly and patted Belinda on her wrinkled kapp. "It will work out. I know it will."

Belinda nodded in agreement. "I know."

Once she was alone, Belinda took out her cell phone from her apron pocket and placed it back in her drawer. It was time to obey her parents no matter how difficult it would be. She simply couldn't go on hurting them like this. Jeff expected too much of her. If he truly loved her, he'd become Amish in a heartbeat. That was for certain.

Lancaster County, Pennsylvania

Late afternoon the next day, Wayne and Josiah came in covered in mud, but Katie chased them out of the house. Then she wiped down the globs of wet dirt from the entryway and clucked her tongue. What were they thinking?

After several minutes, Josiah poked his head around the kitchen door. "We've taken off our shoes and rolled up our trousers. Can we come in so we can change?"

"Nee. Not yet. I'll put some extra clothes on the porch for both of you, and you can change in the barn. Shame on you two!"

She collected clean outfits from the basket she'd just filled from the clothes line, and placed them on a wicker chair outside. Then she spread flour on the counter and took biscuit dough and rolled it out.

Josiah and Wayne looked up as they heard buggy wheels on the drive. They watched as Becky pulled over to the side by the barn.

Josiah waved and called over to say he'd take care of the horse and buggy if she wanted to leave it tethered by the fence near the barn. She gave him a smile and nodded as she climbed down, affixed the reins to the fence and headed towards the kitchen door.

The men reached for the fresh clothes and moved on toward the barn.

"I didn't know we were having company tonight," Josiah said to his brother-in-law. "I was hoping to relax after knocking myself out all day."

"Jah, me too. It should be completed in a couple days, don't you think?"

"Shouldn't take any longer. I appreciate all your help. I know there are a lot of things you'd rather be doing."

"It's fine," said Wayne with a grin. "I like working on things like this. It's challenging."

"Jah, you can say that again."

Becky let herself in the back door and greeted Katie, whose hands were covered in flour as she cut out the biscuits for supper. A tin filled with brownies and fudge was tucked under Becky's arm. She lifted the lid and proudly showed Katie the brownies before setting them aside for dessert. "Does Wayne know I'm staying for supper?"

Katie winked over. "I think I forgot to mention it."

"Josiah looked surprised too, when he saw me. I hope it's all right with him."

"Of course it is. He likes having company and you're the first friend to come for supper. You should feel honored."

"I do. What can I do to help?"

"Just sit and keep me company. I have everything under control. It will be an hour or so before we eat."

Becky pulled out a kitchen chair and sat to watch Katie as she filled a cookie sheet with her biscuits. "Mmm. They look gut."

"I love baking. Now I don't have to worry about my weight. It's easy to stay thin."

"Is that because of the medicine you take?"

"I'm not sure, but my body seems used to it now. I don't have any side affects anymore."

"Oh, that's so gut. Katie, I'm so glad you're doing well. You look ever so pretty again. Your color is bright and pink."

"Jah? That's gut. Did you do any preparation for tomorrow's classes yet?"

"Oh, I finished it earlier. I'm free tonight to relax with my friends. I just hope Wayne sticks around and doesn't get scared off by seeing me here."

"Don't be silly. I'm sure he's happy to see you."

"We'll see. He barely looked over at me."

The door opened and two much cleaner young men appeared at the threshold. "Can we come in now?" Josiah asked with a twinkle in his eyes.

"Oh, stop it. Of course. You two needed a scolding though." She explained about the mud to Becky who grinned over at Wayne.

"If you were our student, we'd make you stay after school."

"Oh jah? And then what? Make me write 'I am a bad boy' a hundred times?"

"Probably." They all laughed and then the men sat down to join Becky at the table.

Josiah spotted the tin Becky had brought and questioned Katie about it.

"That's our dessert tonight. Becky made them. You can peek, but you can't eat any yet."

After taking off the lid, Josiah totally disregarded Katie's warning and broke off a small piece of a brownie and then passed the tin over to Wayne. He grinned and broke off his own piece.

"You two don't listen!" Katie said, placing her fists on her hips. Then she smiled and set up a pot of coffee on the stove. "May as well leave them out and we'll have coffee to go with them. Just don't fill up on dessert and not have room for my meatloaf."

"I always have room for your meatloaf, Katie," Wayne said. "Yours is even better than Mamm's."

"Don't tell her that."

"Nee, I won't. Do you like to cook, Becky?" He looked over at her as he chewed a fresh piece of fudge.

"Oh, jah. I cook all the time at home. My daed says I'm the best cook in the house."

"Goodness, don't let it go to your head. It will swell up like a balloon," Wayne said, his eyes twinkling.

"Nee, I'm not prideful about it. Just thought you'd want to hear."

"Why would I care, Beck?" Wayne's brows rose and his mouth twisted as he held back a grin.

"Mercy, I don't know. Let's talk about something else."

"I like these brownies," Josiah said as he reached for a fresh one. "The fudge looks gut too. Give Katie your recipe, Becky."

"I make gut brownies, don't I?" Katie asked, hurt displayed in her voice.

"Jah, but not as gut as these."

"Hmmph."

"How's school going, Beck? The little monsters behaving?" Wayne pulled at his suspenders and leaned back in his chair.

"Most of the time. Between Kate and me, we keep things under control."

"You have some of our nieces and nephews this year, don't you?"

"Jah, they're the best behaved. Don't you agree Katie?"

"They're pretty gut. My brudders wouldn't put up with shenanigans in their homes."

Wayne kept his eyes on Becky. "I ground up extra venison yesterday. We've stocked our refrigerator. Do you need any, Beck?"

"I'm not sure. I know my daed went hunting last week. I can ask him when I go home."

"Just let me know if you want any. I can drop it off anytime."

"That's nice to offer, Wayne." She gave him her sweetest—saved for special people—smile and Katie noted color rise in her brother's neck. That was a gut sign for sure.

Chapter Fourteen
Holmes County, Ohio

The week dragged for Belinda, though she was busier than usual at the sitting job since Lottie had a spit-up bug and needed changing frequently. Belinda ran a load of clothing each afternoon before leaving for the day.

When she reached home, she would cautiously remove her phone and turn it on long enough to see if Jeff had called and left a message. There had been no calls at all. Each time, she reminded herself she didn't really care, though the next day, the first thing she'd do upon arriving home, was check it again.

Grace was quieter than usual. She rarely smiled, which was unlike her. Belinda knew it was related to her situation and felt added guilt for being the cause of her mother's distress. Even her father seemed subdued and occasionally, she'd notice him study her when he thought she wasn't looking. At least now, she wasn't lying or being deceptive. Heaven knows what would happen though if Jeff suddenly appeared at the door, begging for forgiveness.

When Sunday arrived, it was the visiting week. She had planned to go to a cousin's house two miles up the road since she hadn't seen much of her since she got married a year ago, but Grace asked her to remain home.

"I've invited Zeke to come by and eat dinner with us today. He'd be disappointed if you weren't here."

"Mamm, how could you do that? You know I'm not interested in him or any one else at this point. It will be awkward having him here."

"Just be polite. That's all I'm asking. I'm not suggesting you show him any special interest, but he's a nice young man and he seems to enjoy your company. Come on and help me cut up these beans."

Nellie walked in as they were discussing Zeke. "I wish I was older. I think he's cute. Funny, too."

"I wish you were older, too, Nellie. Then you could have him!" Belinda reached for a paring knife and started cutting off the bean ends.

"You better be nice to him or I'll tell Daed, and then you'll be in big trouble," Nellie said, scowling.

"Listen to her! And you'll be the one to tell, Miss Tattletale?"

"If I have to. Right, Mamm?"

"Now, leave Belinda alone. You'd better watch your manners, young lady. And don't ask nosy questions when Zeke's here."

"Wouldn't think of it," Nellie said indignantly as she slumped onto a kitchen chair.

Belinda's brows met. "Oh right, like the time you asked that old lady if she was pregnant because her tummy stuck out."

"She looked like she was having twins."

"But she had white hair!"

"So? That doesn't mean she's old."

"Well, it's a fairly gut indicator," Belinda said, shaking her head.

"How about the Sing tonight? Will you go with me like you promised?" Nellie asked her sister.

"I guess so. I don't have anything better to do. But I don't want to stay late."

Grace smiled at her daughters. "It will be nice for you to do something together. You always said you liked to sing, Belinda."

"I used to, but I don't have much to sing about right now."

"You have to stop feeling sorry for yourself," Nellie remarked.

"You have too much to say for yourself," Belinda said. "Just wait till you get older and have some adult problems in your life. Now all you have to worry about is whether to wear your blue *frack* or your green one."

"Mamm, tell her to stop! I have problems, too, you know. I'm not a kid anymore. I'm sixteen now."

"Enough, girls. You act like the English—fussing with each other. I expect more from you. Treat each other with love and respect."

Belinda and Nellie looked at each other and Nellie giggled. "Sorry, Mamm. You're right. Let's be friends again Belinda."

"Jah, it's not like we mean it, Mamm, when we argue. It's just kinda fun."

"Well, you wouldn't know it to hear you two. Goodness, I never talked to my schwesters like that. Your sister, Rachel never spoke like that either."

"Jah, Miss Perfect," Belinda said, nodding.

"Mmm. Never a mean word," Nellie added as she rose and put her arm around Belinda's shoulders. "Schwesters forever?"

"Oh, jah. Forever and ever."

Grace shook her head. "You two will be the death of me yet." She joined their laughter.

Zeke arrived exactly at noon, all spiffed up with brand new black trousers and a fresh collarless shirt. His straight brown hair was sleeked back and his face was freshly shaven. Belinda caught a woodsy scent as he shook her hand in greeting. She had to admit, he looked pretty cute.

He suggested a walk since the weather was conducive, having turned warmer overnight. It was in the high sixties and since it hadn't rained in several days, the ground was fairly dry. They walked around the yard and Belinda commented on the clusters of daffodil leaves beginning their journey skyward. Colorful crocus drew their attention. At one point, they needed to step over several large rocks to continue the path. Zeke held her elbow and guided her over. She could have done it with her eyes closed, but she liked the gesture. He was a gentleman. Belinda was surprised at how appealing he could be. He was interested in animal husbandry and read books from the library about it to self-educate himself. She found that surprising, since most of the Amishmen she knew thought they knew all they needed to when they left school in eighth grade.

Perhaps that was one of the things she liked about Jeff—his desire to learn. Once she asked her employers about borrowing books from them and got their permission, she spent time reading when Lottie took her naps and her other chores were done. She was presently reading about English history. As far as American history went, she had learned a lot when she was a student, but she'd never been taught foreign history and it fascinated her.

She brought up the subject and Zeke seemed genuinely interested. He asked several questions, which she was able to answer, and he asked the name of her favorite history book on the subject. He even said he'd check it out of the library the next time he went so he could talk more intelligently about the subject.

When they returned to the house, Nellie had already set the table and mashed the potatoes. Grace checked the roast pork. Zeke offered to help, but Grace suggested he call the others to come to the table instead. He went out to the barn to find Jed and Gideon.

Nellie looked over at her sister. "Like him better now? You're all smiles today."

"Nellie, for goodness sake, please don't question me like this."

"Look, Mamm, she's blushing! She does like him."

Grace looked over and laughed. "You're going to get in trouble, Nellie. Now leave Belinda alone and don't make things up."

"I didn't! She's blushing."

"Nee, I probably got a little sunburn walking around the yard."

"Oh, jah. Sure. Sunburn in March." Nellie poured water into the glasses as she clucked her tongue.

Belinda rolled her eyes at her mother and took her shawl off to hang on the hook. "What can I do to help?"

"Just get the bowls for the vegetables. Everything else is done."

"And I did it," Nellie added.

"I'll clean up then," Belinda suggested.

"Nee, that won't be necessary," Grace said. "You just entertain our guest, is all."

"I'm running out of talk."

"You'll think of something," Nellie said. "You always do."

With that last comment, the three men came through the door and headed to the sink to wash up. Gideon was teasing Zeke about something that happened in the barn. "Did you read about people husbandry too?" Gideon was asking.

"Nee. I think I know all about that one," Zeke said, a grin spread across his face.

Belinda was glad she hadn't been privy to their whole conversation. She looked over at her mother, who was frowning at her husband.

Dinner went well. The conversation was pleasant and shared by the entire group. Nellie behaved herself, much to Belinda's relief. As they sat around the table enjoying their dessert and coffee, the discussion turned to farming, at which point, Belinda allowed her mind to wander. What is Jeff doing at this moment? Did he still go out after church with his friends and sit next to that girl? Her throat began to close up as thoughts of him enjoying the company of another girl took over. Quickly, she turned her attention to the family and forced herself to become involved with the conversation, though rye grass was not a subject that enthralled her.

Zeke looked over once and nodded towards the door. She picked up on his thought and suggested they take a buggy ride to enjoy the unexpectedly warm weather and sunshine.

Once they were on the road, Zeke slowed his horse to an amble. "So how is your English friend, Jeff?"

"Okay, I guess."

"Guess? You don't see him?"

"Not lately."

"Mmm. Are you free to date, Belinda?"

"I'm not interested in dating anyone right now, Zeke. I'm really not."

"But you're not going with that Jeff guy anymore?"

"Nee." It wouldn't be good to have Zeke see tears. She forced herself to look out and concentrate on the scenery.

"Maybe when you decide to date, you'll go out with me sometime. I've liked you for a long time, you know."

"That's very nice of you to say. I'll let you know if I start going out again."

"Gut. In the meantime, I'd like to be your friend."

"You are already."

"I mean a close friend. One you can talk to when you have a problem or someone you can count on to help you out when you need it."

She looked over at his profile. He seemed so sincere. How sweet. "That's nice of you, Zeke. Jah, we can be gut friends and if you need to talk to someone, I'll listen with both my ears."

He reached over and patted her hand and then replaced his hand on the reins. They rode in silence for a few moments and then he pulled over to point out a herd of deer off in a meadow. They watched as the deer grazed. "Lovely, aren't they?" Belinda said.

"Jah, sometimes it's hard for me to kill them, but one has to eat and there are so many deer that starve over the winter."

"True. As long as it's not just for sport, but for food, I think I understand, though I could never shoot one myself. I don't even like to watch the slaughtering."

"Nee, I wouldn't imagine you would. You're a tender girl, I'm thinking."

She smiled over. "Not always, just ask Nellie."

He laughed. "She's a cute girl. My brother Justin thinks she's going to be his future wife."

Belinda looked at him and giggled. "My, he's certainly looking ahead."

"He just turned sixteen. That's about the age I was when I started noticing you."

"Goodness. That was a while ago."

"Jah. So shall we move on?"

"Gut idea. I love the sunshine. I'm so glad it will be spring soon."

"Maybe we can plan a picnic when it's warmer. Just the two of us."

"That sounds a little like a date."

"Maybe we'll include Justin and Nellie and then it won't be."

Belinda laughed. It felt so good to have laughter replace tears. "We'll see."

After an hour they returned and it was decided that the three of them, Belinda, Zeke and Nellie, would ride together to the Sing in Zeke's buggy.

When they arrived at the barn where the Sing was held, everyone seemed excited to see her again. It was good to be out with her friends. It had been way too long and she promised she'd try to come to every Sing and Frolic in the future.

On the way to bed that night, she realized she was still humming a tune. Her life wasn't over just because one guy didn't find her worth changing his religion for. And why should he? Changing your beliefs for someone else is wrong and no one should expect it. Not even when you loved someone. As she settled her head onto her pillow, she closed her eyes and pictured the whole evening. Then Jeff's face appeared to her. Quickly, she thought about someone else. That someone was Zeke. She smiled and fell asleep before she had time to analyze her thoughts.

Chapter Fifteen
Lancaster County, Pennsylvania

Time went quickly now that Katie had her teaching position back. It was already April and she saw little of Josiah until supper time since he had his fields to work. His brothers sometimes came over to help and in return, he'd assist them with their heavier chores from time to time.

Katie loved being married. She knew God had blessed her life with a wonderful man, a Godly man, who did everything humanly possible to make her happy. She found fresh wild flowers on the table sometimes in the morning when she came down to prepare his breakfast. Occasionally, he'd write a short love note and place it next to her dust rag or plate to surprise her. Everything was perfect. Well, perhaps not quite. The monthly reminder of her inability to be a mother, placed a pall on her otherwise wonderful life, but she spent time in prayer at those times and came away counting her blessings.

Katie and Belinda kept up their friendship through the mail. They wrote to each other every week to keep up with the news. Katie learned of Belinda's break-up with Jeff and spoke to Josiah about it. "They were so in love. I feel sorry for her," she said one evening as they relaxed together on the sofa.

Josiah nodded. "It would be real hard to give someone up like that. Jeff's probably thinking of her best interests in the end. If he wasn't going to become Amish, it would have been unfair to marry her and take her away from her family and friends."

"Could you have done that? Give me up for my own good, kind of?"

"I don't know. I know when we weren't getting along, I was miserable. No one wanted to be around me. I didn't even want to be around me," he said as he pulled her closer to him. "But thankfully, everything is gut now and nothing can tear us apart."

"I was pretty stubborn for a while, wasn't I?" Katie asked, grinning.

"Mmm. You could say that," he answered, returning a smile. "Are you glad it's Friday and you have off from teaching for two days?"

"In a way, though I love to teach. I have a lot to catch up on here at home. I want to plant more peas and lettuce before it gets too warm."

"The early lettuce is already coming along gut. You can pick some soon for our salads."

"Jah, I know. Maybe tomorrow for supper I'll make a big salad."

"Katie, what else did the doctor tell you about your last blood tests?"

"Nothing much. Just that I'm still free of cancer. What a wonderful feeling."

"I bet. Honey, I know you were upset the other day when you, you know, had your monthly. I just want you to know, that I'm not expecting anything to happen. It doesn't matter to me. As long as you're okay, nothing else is important. Please keep that in mind so you won't be disappointed every month."

"I know you're right. It's hard, is all. But I've accepted it. I think it helps to be with kinner all week. In fact, by the end of the week, it's nice to come home just to you."

"That's my Katie-girl. Now let me check the animals and we'll get to bed early. Tomorrow's another busy day for your farmer husband." He kissed her and headed out the back door.

Holmes County, Ohio

Belinda positioned Lottie in her bouncy seat while she folded baby clothes and placed them in the dresser. Madison would be home in the next few minutes, though she saw little of her. Good thing she had Vera to take over the care of the baby when she had to leave.

As she put the last of the knitted sweaters away, she heard Madison head up the stairs. She poked her head in the nursery door and said hi. There was no friend with her today and she looked tired.

"Hi. Come on in. Your sister cut her first tooth today."

"Oh yeah?" Madison knelt by Lottie's seat and stuck her index finger on Lottie's gum. The baby gave a drooly grin and Madison smiled back. Then she wiped her finger on her jeans.

"No friend today?" Belinda asked.

"Everyone had somewhere to go. It's okay. I'm gonna take a nap anyway. You don't need me, do you?"

"I guess Vera can handle things. She usually does. I'll be leaving in a couple minutes."

"Can I ask you something?"

"Sure. What?"

"How can you stand being Amish? I mean, you lead such boring lives. I don't mean to…that is, I guess maybe you don't think it's boring, but…"

"It's okay. I'm sure it looks boring to people on the outside, but the truth is, we lead such busy lives, we don't have time to be bored. It's better than it looks."

"What about guys?"

"What about them?"

"Well, do you go out and you know…"

"We date before we're married, sure."

"Do you have sex with them?"

Belinda's mouth dropped. "My goodness, you certainly ask strange questions."

Madison laughed and shook her head. "I guess that was rude."

"Jah, a little. But to answer your question, we are careful before we marry. Sex is something for husbands and wives, not single people."

"I don't know how you do it. Like wait."

"It's too important to just go around kissing and stuff with any guy you like at the moment. It's not supposed to be that way. When we marry, it's real special. It's a God thing. It's like when two people promise to live together for life, and love each other no matter what, they've spoken before God. It's not something they can break."

"Wow. You really believe all that stuff?"

"Of course. I'm sorry you don't. You should be careful, though. You could get a disease or wreck your life."

"That's so quaint. Listen, I'm sorry if I offended you, I've just been curious."

"It's okay. Really. I don't mind talking about it. For a while I went with an English guy. In fact, we only broke up recently. We were really in love and it's been tough."

"Why did you break up?"

"I guess it was because of our families. We really are living in different worlds. I just couldn't give up being Amish and he couldn't become Amish, so that was that."

"I bet it was hard."

"The hardest thing I've ever been through."

"You sound like you still care."

"I guess I do, but I try not to think about him."

"Listen, you can leave. I'll watch Lottie today. I don't have anything better to do."

"You sure? Vera's downstairs and I can—"

"No, I should help out a little. Besides, she's kinda cute. If she cries, I'll take her down to Vera."

"Okay. She just ate an hour ago, so she should be okay for awhile."

"Do I just leave her in that seat? Can I take her out?"

"Sure. You can hold her if you want."

"I'll wait until she fusses. Thanks, Belinda."

Belinda smiled as she gathered her shawl and headed toward the door. "Bye Madison, bye Lottie. See you both tomorrow." The baby cooed and chewed on her fist.

As she walked home, Belinda inhaled deeply. Spring was in full force and it was one of those days when it felt good just to be alive. The warmth from the sun, the blossoming trees,—what more could you ask for?

She was shocked to see Carrie's car in the driveway when she arrived home. She licked her dry lips and swallowed hard as thoughts ran through her head. Was Jeff with her? Was he ill? Did he want to reconcile?

When she came through the kitchen door, Carrie was having tea with Nellie and her mother. She looked up and smiled as Belinda closed the door behind her.

"Carrie, it's gut to see you. I hope everything is okay," Belinda said as she removed her shawl.

"Want tea, dochder?" Grace asked.

"Sure. When did you get here?" Belinda asked as she sat next to her friend.

"She's been here a whole hour," Nellie offered before Carrie had a chance to speak.

Grace set a cup and saucer in front of Belinda and poured from the teapot. Butterscotch cookies sat in the middle of the table.

"I've just missed you, Belinda, and I wondered how you were doing."

"That's nice. I've missed you too. How is Jeff?" She tried to keep her tone indifferent, as if she was merely asking about a friend, while her heart was beating wildly as she waited for the answer.

"Busy. Always busy. The only time we see each other is on Sunday. I go to the Mennonite Meetinghouse now with him."

"I see. You're still in college?"

"Yeah. This is our spring break. I go back Sunday night."

"Have another cookie, Carrie," Grace said, her voice strained. Belinda sensed her mother's fear and concern at having Jeff's sister turn up, but at least she had been civil and invited her to stay for awhile. She was rather proud of her mother for not forgetting to be hospitable.

"No, I should really be getting home. I'm going out with a friend tonight to a concert."

"That's nice. We won't hold you up." Grace stood and went to place her own cup and saucer in the sink.

"You don't have to leave quite yet, do you?" Belinda asked.

"Not until my tea is finished. It's really good tea, Mrs. Glick."

"It's just Red Rose. We always buy the same."

"Well, thank you."

Nellie poured more tea into her cup and stared over at their guest. "Is Jeff going out with anyone?"

Belinda took in a sharp breath. Surely, she hadn't heard right.

Carrie's brows arched. "Well, I don't know, Nellie. I don't think so."

"My sister went to a sing with a guy."

"Nellie, why don't you go feed the cats," Belinda said pointedly.

"I already did."

"Well, I guess I'd better get home. It's getting late." Carrie rose and reached for her sweater and purse, which were sitting on a vacant chair next to her.

"I'll walk you to your car," Belinda said, staring down her sister, just daring her to say anything further.

When they got to the car, Carrie stood by the driver's side. "I'm sorry everything has fallen apart for you and Jeff. I know how much you guys loved each other. It has to be difficult."

"It's been rough, I won't deny that," Belinda said, choking on her words. "You can tell me the truth, Carrie. Is Jeff dating someone else?"

She looked down at the door handle and sucked in her cheeks. "It's nothing serious. He just gets together with one of the Mennonite girls once in a while. I think he still cares for you, Belinda, but at this point it doesn't look like it will work out for you two."

"I know. I still care—too much, but I have to move on and so does he. I'm just sorry it had to end in anger."

"He doesn't talk much about it anymore. I may not even tell him I stopped by. I'm not sure what to do."

"Would he be angry if he knew?"

"I doubt it, but then he'd ask me tons of questions and I'm not sure he'd appreciate hearing the answers."

"Nell is such a brat sometimes. My 'date' was barely that. Zeke is more of a gut friend than anyone I'd ever be serious about."

"It doesn't matter. No one would expect you to wait forever for Jeff to know what he's doing. He still goes and talks to some Amish guy he's befriended, but we don't talk about it. Not anymore."

"I hope he'll be happy someday, even if it's not with me. He's a great guy." Belinda felt a tear trickle down her cheek and she wiped it away with her sleeve.

Carrie reached across and gave her a hug. "I'm sorry. I'll keep in touch." Then she got in the car and Belinda watched as she made her way down the drive to the road. They waved at each other as she turned down the street towards her home. It was final now. Belinda knew in her heart it was over. She walked slowly back to the house and went directly to her room. Nellie was not in sight, much to

Belinda's relief. She'd have to rid herself of her anger and it would take God to help her do so. For sure and for certain.

Chapter Sixteen
Holmes County, Ohio

Jeff turned his church bulletin over and wrote notes on the edges as the minister gave his sermon on the beatitudes. A separate sheet fell onto the floor and as he reached down his hand grazed the side of Megan's leg. His heart jumped as he became aware of her womanliness. As he settled back in his seat, he tried to concentrate on the sermon.

His sister sat on his left and Randy sat on the aisle seat next to Carrie. There were several of their friends seated in the pew in front of them. His life was so full—between school, work, and church, it left him little time to stress over Belinda. At times like this though, he felt the void in his life. He knew it was probably wise to stay apart. After all, there seemed to be no solution for them as a couple and to prolong their relationship, knowing there was no easy resolution, seemed foolhardy. And yet...

Jeff looked over at Megan. She was rising from the pew, along with everyone else in the congregation. He hadn't even realized the sermon was over. He stood up as the a cappella chorale group gathered at the front for the final song. After the last prayer, the people began to move from their seats and head for the exits, though his group gathered at the back of the sanctuary to make plans for lunch. Megan smiled at Jeff and told him she thought he'd fallen asleep once.

"Almost. It was warm in here."

"I thought so, too. Are you joining us for hoagies?"

"Sure."

"Good. You can leave your car here and go with me. Cindy and Joel are going with me, too."

"Will you be coming back this way afterward? I don't want you to go out of your way for me."

"I'll be passing right by. I'm taking cake over to Mrs. Kinsey this afternoon. She loves my spice cake and I want to take her the bulletin."

"I don't know her. Does she come here?"

"She used to before she broke her hip. Now she's bedridden at the nursing home, but they're hoping she'll one day return to her own home."

"Want company?"

"How nice of you to ask. Sure. The men would love some young blood to show up. Maybe you can play checkers or something with some of them while I visit the women. The cake is huge and should feed all the residents, as well as staff."

"Okay. I won't refuse a piece. Spice cake is one of my favorites."

Once everyone was informed of the eating place, groups headed out. When they arrived at the hoagie shop, some of the group had pushed tables together. There were sixteen gathered around to share lunch.

What a pleasant change from the group Jeff used to hang out with in school. No foul language, no overt sexual overtures, not even heavy sarcasm. Some teasing and lots of laughter. He never regretted his decision to join the Mennonites. He even enjoyed driving his black car now. He missed nothing about his previous life. Nothing, except a lovely Amish woman. But he wouldn't go there. Not today.

Lancaster County, Pennsylvania

Becky stopped by Katie and Josiah's house on Saturday to drop off test papers for Katie to mark and ended up staying for supper. After they ate, Josiah went out to the barn to check the animals and Becky dried the dishes while Katie washed. The subject came up about Wayne, as it usually did.

"Does your brudder ever talk about me?"

"Nee, but he doesn't talk about any girls, so it doesn't mean anything."

"We've been getting along better than ever. I was kinda hoping he'd ask me to go out with him by now."

"I think he's afraid to get serious."

"Goodness, we're not getting any younger," she commented as she placed the dishes in a cupboard. He's eighteen now. He should be thinking about his future wife."

"He's got plenty of time, Becky. Why the rush? You like teaching, right?"

"I do, but I sure would like a boyfriend. Maybe I don't need to get married yet, but it would be ever so much fun to have a guy interested in me."

"There are other guys, you know."

"Not for me. You know how I feel about Wayne. I try to like other guys, but it just doesn't happen."

"I can't believe it. Wayne, of all people. He's so immature." Katie put the last pot in the drain and wiped her hands on a towel.

"Not anymore, Katie. You don't see him as he really is." Becky dried the pot and set the dishtowel on the towel bar. The girls stepped over to the table.

Katie smiled. "Perhaps you're right," she said as she and Becky sat down. "I know too much about him."

"But if you weren't his sister—"

"Beck, he is! I can't pretend otherwise."

"How can I get to see him again without being too obvious?"

"Well, we're going over to Mamm's tomorrow after church service. You could stop by to pick up these tests."

"Don't you think he'd figure out we were using it as an excuse?"

"Wayne doesn't try to analyze anything. He wouldn't even give it a second thought. Jah, come join us and maybe you can get him off to yourself for awhile. I'll try to think of some way."

"Danki. It's worth a try. I just finished sewing a new frack last night. It's a pretty pale green dress. I think I'll wear that tomorrow."

"You could come home with us after the service and then you'd have no way to get home so he'd have to take you. What do you think?"

"And if he didn't offer?"

"Then I'd take you, but I think he will. He's a gentleman, sometimes."

"He is, Katie. A real gentleman. I don't know what I'll do if he marries someone else. I might never get married to anyone if that happens."

"Don't be silly. Goodness, there are a lot of nice guys in our district. You've been asked out."

"Jah, but the last time I went to a Frolic with a guy, he ended up flirting the whole time with Priscilla."

"That girl! I wish she'd either move or get married to someone. She's not happy unless she's charming some guy."

"I think she's fast."

"What does that mean?"

"You know," Becky said, tilting her head close to Katie's. "Like too free with the guys."

"Could be. Thankfully, Josiah didn't fall for her."

"Jah, and she was after him, everyone could see that."

"You don't think…"

"Nee. He was too smitten with you to fall for her shenanigans. You know better than to doubt that."

"I worried for awhile, but not anymore. We're so happy. He's a wonderful-gut man."

"Jah, you've been blessed, Katie. At least with your husband, maybe not your health."

"Well, I'm free of cancer now anyway and hope to remain that way."

"Katie, I don't like to ask something that might upset you…"

"But?"

"But, are you gonna have boppli, do you think? You don't have to answer, if I'm out of line, but you are my best friend and all."

"It's okay. Let's put it this way. We aren't trying real hard, but if it happens, it would be ever so nice."

"And the leukemia?"

"I'd have to go off the medication till the baby is born."

"Would that put you at risk?"

"Somewhat."

"I'd be scared to then. Ever think of adoption?"

"We've talked about it and I've put word out with my family in case they hear of a case where someone is trying to find adoptive parents. It ain't easy to find in the Amish community."

"Nee. I know. I'll keep my ears open, too, just in case."

Katie stretched her arms above her head. "We should go for a walk. It's nice and warm out."

"I'll take my shawl," Becky said as she stood to follow Katie to the back door."

As they walked around the yard, Becky asked her about Belinda.

"She's not seeing Jeff anymore. It still hurts her, but she realized it wasn't going to work without leaving the Amish and she couldn't do that."

"What a shame. I'd never date an Englisher, just for that reason. Why take a chance on getting hurt."

"I agree. It's not smart. She sees a guy named Zeke, but she says he's more of a friend than anything else."

"Maybe Jeff will turn Amish for her."

"I asked her that, but she said his family's even upset that he turned Mennonite. Just think if he bought himself a buggy!"

"Oh jah, what indeed!"

After their walk, Becky left for her home while Katie took a short nap. Her energy level was still not up to par, but each week, she felt progress.

Chapter Seventeen
Holmes County, Ohio

Lottie cut two more lower teeth and attempted to sit up now, having turned five months on May first. She wasn't strong enough to actually sit by herself, but she was determined to succeed and fussed if on her back too long. She'd turn over onto her tummy and arch herself up with her arms.

Madison made herself available several times a week now to take over when it was time for Belinda to leave for home. She seemed to enjoy her talks with her new Amish friend, and Belinda was glad for the company. She often stayed on for another hour to chat. Sometimes the girls laid on the floor with Lottie between them and handed her toys to chew on while they gabbed.

"I haven't seen you with that guy, Cab, lately. Don't you like him?" Belinda asked one afternoon.

"He's okay. We're not going together anymore, though."

"That's too bad, I guess. How did he get his name?"

"When he was little he lived in Manhattan with his parents and he was fascinated by the yellow cabs. They started calling him Cabbie and it stuck. When he got older it was shortened to Cab."

"It must be hard to live in a big city."

"His parents broke up and his mother took off. He ended up living here with his grandmother."

"That's a shame. Does he see his father?"

"About once every couple years. They have no relationship."

"And his mother?"

"He doesn't even talk about her. He hates discussing his family, so I just stay clear of the subject."

"I'm glad you have parents who care," Belinda said as she pulled the baby back onto the quilt after she rolled off.

"I can't stand Deb. She hates me."

"Nee, how could she hate you?"

"Just watch the way she talks to me some day. You'll see."

"Surely your daed loves you."

"I guess, though I don't see that much of either one of them." She poked her sister in the tummy and she giggled back. "I feel sorry for Lottie."

"That's a shame they have to work such long hours."

"They don't need to. It's their choice. I'm never gonna have kids. It's too much work and they always get screwed up."

"Not true, Madison. You seem okay in spite of everything you've gone through."

"Oh, I'm messed up, too. Big time. I guess I wanted to grow up too fast."

"What are your plans when you graduate high school?"

"I don't have anything definite in mind. My father expects me to go to college, but I have no idea what I want to be. Probably a druggie."

Belinda looked up and saw a crooked grin on Madison's face. "Oh, merciful day, I thought you were serious."

"I'm not that dumb. I don't believe in taking drugs. Not illegal ones, anyway. That's where Cab and I part company. He'll try anything to get high."

"So foolish. I don't understand it. I know an Amish guy who smoked pot once and he said it was disgusting."

"Lucky for him, he has a head on his shoulders."

"Are you gonna go out with any other guys now that you broke off with Cab?"

"Maybe. Tonight there's a party at one of my girlfriends. I'll probably go, if the witch let's me."

"I hope she will. I know what it's like to be kept at home." Belinda proceeded to tell her about her experiences attending parties with the English. She even told her all about Jeff and how she still loved him, though she knew now it would never end up in a real relationship.

"You should turn English then."

"I can't leave my family. My mother would be crushed. So would my daed and my sisters and brother. It's too much to do to people who love you. I'd probably be banned, you know."

"That's nuts. What does it matter?"

"It's the way we've been able to keep our culture alive. We can't make exceptions or pretty soon everyone would be doing their own thing and probably even divorcing."

"They don't divorce? Ever?"

"It's against our faith. That's one reason we're so careful about who we date. You don't get a second chance."

"Wow. That's scary."

Belinda laughed. "I think I'd better head home now. I want to do some weeding tonight before it gets dark. It's too much for my mother to do it all herself."

"You're really a nice daughter, Belinda. I should take lessons."

"Why don't you come over and meet my family some time," Belinda suggested.

"Really? I'd love to. I don't know what I'd wear though."

Belinda giggled. "They'd know you weren't Amish. You just wear whatever you have on." Belinda noted how Madison's knit blouse was stretched tightly across her bosom and added, "You might want to wear something a little looser though."

It was Madison's turn to laugh. "I get it. Don't show it off, right?"

"Something like that," Belinda answered, smiling back. "I have a brother who might pass out if he saw a girl like you at the house."

Lottie let out a cry and Madison picked her up. "I'll take you up on that some day. Just give me time to buy a size extra-large sweater first."

Belinda kissed Lottie on the head and went downstairs while Madison placed the baby on the changing table to put fresh diapers on her.

Lancaster County, Pennsylvania

After the church service, the Zooks all gathered for the afternoon at the parents' homestead. Oma was in her glory with all the grandchildren and great-grandkids in attendance. Gabe and Emma's daughter, Lizzy, made a big fuss over the elderly lady and gave her a paper bracelet she'd made along with another poem. Lizzie also played with the twin girls, giving her mother a chance to visit with her sisters, Ruth and Katie.

Their brothers Mark and Isaac showed up with their families and the house burst with conversation and laughter. Becky had returned from church with Katie, as planned, and she and Wayne sat at the end of the living room on the floor and chatted. Katie looked over at her friend and was elated to see she and her brother were hitting it off. She heard him laugh and once caught him poke Becky on her kapp. All signs of attention. Wouldn't it be tremendous to have Becky as her sister-in-law!

Oma motioned for Katie to come to her side. When she moved over and sat in the chair next to her grandmother, Oma asked about Belinda.

"She's doing okay, but she's real upset."

"Goodness, why?"

"It's not working out with Jeff."

"That nice young Englisher who came here to help?"

"Jah. He is nice, but she doesn't want to leave the Amish community."

"Well, mercy no. Why doesn't he yank over to the Amish?"

"Oma, it's not that easy, I guess. It's probably harder for someone to give up a lot of stuff than for someone to leave the Amish and have life a lot easier."

"Easier physically maybe, but my, they have their problems. My friend was over last week to see me and she knows an Englisher who's divorced three times. That's just so sad."

"Jah, but some of them don't think anything of it."

"I'm glad Belinda didn't leave her family. Grace and Jed would have been heartbroken."

"You're right about that. Nee, she made the right choice if you ask me. Besides, she kind of likes an Amishman now and apparently he really likes her."

Oma nodded her head with fervor. "That's gut. Much better. Maybe we'll have a wedding to attend before long. I love weddings. They're ever so much fun."

Katie smiled in agreement.

"Are you in a family way yet, Katie?"

Her smile turned down and she felt her depression crash down on her. It was difficult enough to keep her mind off pregnancy and boppli, and now here the subject popped up again.

"Nee, it may not happen, Oma. Because of the leukemia and the medicine I'm on."

"Oh, my. I shouldn't have asked. I'm sorry sweetheart. I remember now, Mary told me about that. It's okay, though. Not everyone has to have boppli. There are plenty who do, so our community won't fade away."

"It's not like I don't want one."

Oma reached over and patted her hand. "I know. *Es dutt mir leed.*"

"I know you're sorry. Please don't feel bad. Lots of people have questioned me."

Oma's eyes filled. "My *liebschdi*. My dear child."

Katie wrapped her arms around Oma and the two shared a tender, though painful moment. Katie thanked God for her grandmother and the fact she was still amongst them. It helped her ever so much to have her love.

Chapter Eighteen
Holmes County, Ohio

Belinda was true to her word and invited Madison to come by for dinner the following Saturday. When she arrived, Belinda noted she had on a large somber grey sweater and somewhat loose jeans. She wondered if she'd borrowed them since they looked two sizes too big. Even her eye make-up was toned down for the occasion.

At first it was awkward. Conversation seemed forced, but Gideon told a couple stories that got everyone smiling and soon Belinda noticed Madison seemed more like herself. After they ate, she insisted on helping clean the kitchen though Grace tried to discourage her. Afterward, Belinda took her around the property and showed her the barn. Madison clamped her nose shut with her hand, which amused Belinda. "I guess I'm just used to the odor," she said as they exited quickly.

"I don't know how you stand it. Do you know how to milk those cows?"

"Of course," Belinda said, holding back a giggle. "Every Amish girl learns to milk. We all work the farm. It's too much for just daed and my brother."

"Do you like doing it?"

"I don't know if I like it. I just do it, is all. It's part of my responsibility."

"You're amazing. I like your family, Belinda. They seem real."

Belinda couldn't hold back her laughter any longer. "Mercy, we're all real—really!"

Madison saw the humor and joined Belinda in laughing. "I guess that was silly to say. It's just that I've never actually spent time with Amish. They always appeared so somber and grumpy."

"Oh jah, I can be real grumpy sometimes, but we have lots of fun times, too. I love my family with all my heart."

"You must, to give up a man because of them."

"I just wish I could get over him. It's been so hard."

"I know what you mean. I'm still upset over Cab. We were close and I thought he really cared."

"Maybe he'll come back to you."

"I doubt it." Madison stopped walking and leaned against the fence by the horse corral. "He's going out with another girl, who used to be my best friend. So much for friends."

"That's a shame."

"I hope she has a heart attack or something."

"Madison! That ain't proper to think that."

Madison turned and smiled. "I guess I don't mean it."

"I hope not. Goodness, you have to be forgiving."

"Why? I think it rots to take another girl's boyfriend."

"It's wrong, but God wants us to love—even our enemies."

"Sure. Like you can."

"If you choose to, it's possible. But it's not easy. You need God to help you with anger and hate and stuff like that."

"I guess I'm not even sure if there is a God." She leaned over and patted one of the horses on his head. He enjoyed the attention and hung out near the railing.

"Don't you ever go to church?" Belinda asked.

"No one in the family does. I've only been in church two times in my whole life and that was for a wedding once and a Christmas play the other time. I went with a friend."

"You can come with me sometime, but you wouldn't understand much. It's mostly in *Deitsch*."

"Oh yeah. You can speak a different language, can't you?"

"Jah. That's what I learned first, even before English. Most kinner learn it at home."

"That's cool. I wish I could speak another language."

"Don't you learn to in school?"

"I took two years of French, but I can't speak it. Maybe read a little, but that's it. Well, I guess I'd better head home. I have a lot of homework." They walked back to the house where Madison went in first to thank Grace for the meal.

"I hope you'll come back again to see us, Madison. We enjoyed having you."

"I love your cooking, Mrs. Glick. Vera's good, but you're way better."

Grace laughed and Belinda noticed a blush on her mother's neck. She wasn't used to compliments.

After Madison left, Belinda went up to her room and wrote to Katie. She told her about the day and how Madison couldn't stand the smell of the barn. She knew Katie would get a chuckle out of that. It surprised her that Madison had changed so since she'd opened up to her. She really seemed to need a friend. Poor girl didn't have much family life. Lots of things—lots of money, but how empty her home life seemed. Jah, she was the poor one, after all. Maybe she could spend more time with Belinda and her family to help fill the void. And just maybe, Belinda could help her find her way to God. That would be ever so gut.

Lancaster County, Pennsylvania

"Look at you," Mary exclaimed as her mother walked around the kitchen without her walker. "I can't believe how much you've improved."

"I made up my mind I'm going to be independent again. I want to move into the dawdi haus real soon and then you can get on with your life, dochder."

Mary shook her head. "I'm just fine the way things are, but I can understand how you feel. Just take your time. It's all furnished already from your house you know. You've seen it."

"Many times. It feels like home already when I peek in. I'm thinking I'll move in next week-end, if Leroy can just move my clothing over there."

"I'm sure he can. If not, Wayne will do it. You should still have all your meals with us though, Mamm."

"Except breakfast. I like to eat a little later than you do and I don't mind making my own oatmeal. I like it smoother than you make it."

Mary laughed. "Mercy, why didn't you tell me? I could have cooked it longer for you."

"I don't like complaining. You were gut enough to make it every day. Why should I fuss?"

"The family will be surprised to see how much you've improved in such a short time."

"Jah, and I'll take my own shower from now on. No more tub baths."

"That is a nice shower in there. Now that you can stand on your own, I guess it would be all right. Leroy wants to add a couple more safety bars for you to hold onto first. He can do it this week. He already bought them."

"He's such a fine son-in-law. I don't know what I'd do without him. Without any of you. You're a true blessing, dochder."

Mary took a step closer and put her arms around her mother. "I'm the one blessed—to have you for a mudder."

Becky filled Katie in on her conversations with Wayne from their day together the past Sunday. The children were outside for their break and Becky talked a mile a minute about her day. "He laughed at my jokes, Katie. Even the dumb ones."

"I notice he seems to be happy a lot."

"Jah, and he talked about having a picnic next week. Just the two of us. Katie, I think he's beginning to like me."

"He's always liked you."

"You know what I mean. *Really* like me. Like a girlfriend."

"Now don't get your hopes too high. My brudder is kind of fickle. He talks about a different girl every week, it seems."

"He's getting older, Katie. He needs to settle down soon."

"Jah? You tell him that. He thinks he's Mr. Wonderful Single Guy."

"He is!"

"Oh, Becky. Who do you see when you look at my brudder? Surely not the guy I see."

"Schwesters aren't the best judge you know. After all, I'm sure he's different around the family. Around me, he's really special now. I hope I'm not wrong about his feelings, but he doesn't take girls on private picnics everyday, does he?"

"Nee, not every day, but you aren't the first."

"Don't tell me anymore. I don't want to hear it."

"Don't get mad at me."

Becky laughed. "Nee, I'm not, but I don't want my hopes shattered."

"Just remember I warned you about him." After checking the clock, Katie went to the door and called the children back in. With the warm weather, it was getting harder all the time to keep the children settled down enough to do their work.

Only three more weeks of school. Katie was relieved. It was time to spend more time at her own place now with the gardens producing and more planting to be done.

Besides, she missed Josiah when she was teaching all day. After all, they were still on their honeymoon as far as she was concerned. She marked the calendar as the children took their seats. Fourteen school days left. Then she opened the teacher's book and took her place with the students.

Chapter Nineteen
Holmes County, Ohio

Belinda dressed Lottie in a sundress and matching hat and took her outside in her stroller. She pushed it back and forth along the driveway. May was Belinda's favorite month of the year and today the sky was as blue as she'd ever seen it, with only wisps of clouds skirting across the horizon. Lottie sat propped up as she chewed on her fist. She bounced forward when she spotted a squirrel only two feet from the stroller scooting up a large maple tree.

Belinda watched as the school bus arrived across the street. Lottie's attention was drawn to the noisy vehicle. When her big sister stepped down and headed their way, Lottie let out little squeals of excitement and strained to sit taller.

Madison's expression concerned Belinda. She had a deep frown and her eyes were lowered. She barely noticed Lottie.

"Hi, Madison. How was school?" Belinda asked, hoping to lighten her mood.

"The usual. Boring. I have to pee. I'll talk to you later." She walked quickly toward the house and slammed the front door behind her. Lottie went back to her chewing and tugged on a cotton blanket as she did so. When they returned to the house, Belinda laid her down for her nap and talked to Vera about listening for the baby so she could leave.

As they spoke, Madison came into the kitchen, reached for a gallon of skim milk, and poured herself a glassful. She glanced over at Belinda and Vera. "It's okay. I can take care of her. I feel better now."

Vera nodded. "You're getting to be quite the young sitter, Madison. See? Babies ain't so bad after all."

Madison's eyes filled unexpectedly. Vera's attention was on a bundt cake she was icing, and only Belinda noticed the change in Madison. She followed her out to the hallway and touched her shoulder.

"What?" Madison's voice pierced the air.

"Sorry," Belinda said, taken aback, "I just wondered if you were okay."

"Why wouldn't I be?"

"You tell me. I know you well enough to know you're upset about something. Wanna talk? I don't have to run off yet."

"Not really. I just have to make a major decision about something."

"College?"

"Hardly. Oh, I may as well tell you. It won't be long before the whole world will know. I'm pregnant."

Belinda felt a rush of air leave her as she gasped. "No way."

"Oh, yeah way. Cab's kid."

"I figured. Does he know?"

"Let's go to my room. I don't want Vera to hear. She's got a big mouth and I don't want my parents to find out."

They walked up and went directly into her bedroom, closing the door behind them.

"Sit on the bed next to me," Madison suggested.

Belinda smoothed out her skirt and sat near the end of the bed beside her.

"So, to answer your question, no, he doesn't know and I don't want him to find out."

"It will be obvious eventually. Why not talk to him now about it. I'm sure he'd want to marry you."

Madison let out a painful laugh. "Right. It doesn't work that way anymore, Belinda. Not in my world. This is *my* problem."

"Oh, goodness. It will be hard on you. Will you quit school?"

"School's almost over now. I've got another year before I graduate. I plan to do just that—graduate."

"That's gut. I can watch your baby along with Lottie."

"There's not going to be a baby, Belinda. I'm getting rid of it as soon as I find a way."

"Nee, you're kidding, right?"

"I've never been so serious." Her eyes began to fill again.

Belinda moved closer and put her arm around her friend's shoulders. "Don't do anything so drastic without praying about it. It's already a little boppli, you know that."

"Pray? I don't think so. He's not going to listen to my prayers. Besides, girls have abortions all the time. It's no big deal."

"You don't really believe that in your heart, do you?"

"Belinda, this isn't going to help matters. I'm too young to be pregnant. I certainly don't need a kid right now. Maybe someday, but certainly not at this stage of my life."

"Why not talk to your father about it. It's a big step, Madison. A huge step."

"He'd kill me."

"Really?" Belinda's brows rose.

"Well, not really, but he'd be furious. He wouldn't care if I got an abortion."

"You don't know that."

"He'd be cool about it, I'm sure. I don't know about Deb though. She'd be upset either way because it would look bad for her with her club crowd to have her step-daughter get pregnant."

"Maybe my mother would raise your child. She loves kinner."

"Belinda, get with it. Don't you see, I don't want to get fat and ugly. Pregnant women end up having babies, you know. I've heard horrible things about delivering. I'm not about to go through all that for nothing. I wouldn't keep it at any cost."

"But it's a life! It's too late to wish it wasn't so. How far along are you?"

"I just missed my second period. I didn't want to believe it, but I can't deny it anymore. I used a kit from the drug store and it came out positive. Sometimes I throw up in the morning, too. Real fun."

"I'm so sorry."

Madison's eyes widened. "Why are you sorry? You didn't do anything."

"I consider you a friend. I hate to see you go through all this."

"It'll be over soon. I have a friend who's older and I know she had an abortion a couple years ago. I'm going to call her later today. Just pretend you never heard about it and we won't talk about it again. Look, I appreciate you caring the way you do, but this is my decision. I'll live with it."

"What if Deb had aborted Lottie? Can you imagine if she had been destroyed?"

That got to her. She burst into tears and shook her head. "That's not fair. You're playing on my emotions. Lottie's different. She has parents and us. My baby would have nothing. No one."

"That's not true. There are couples who would love to adopt your baby. Please, don't do anything yet. Promise you'll wait a little while till you're sure of your decision. It's early yet. You have time. Please."

Madison looked up at Belinda through her tears. "You really care that much? Okay, I'll hold off for a week or so, though nothing's going to change."

"Danki. Thank you for listening. Please pray about it. God will hear you. He loves you, you know, even if you don't even believe in him. He created you just as he's creating a new life in you right at this very moment."

"It's just a blob of tissue, Belinda. Don't get your facts messed up."

"Do me a favor. You have a computer. Go to it after I leave and look up fetus. Read about it, Madison. You'll be amazed, I guarantee it. When my sister found out she was pregnant, we went to the library and checked it out. I couldn't believe what I read."

"If I have time, I'll check it out. I don't know if I really want to know."

"Don't make such a major decision blindly. You'll someday regret it."

Madison stared over at Belinda. Her eyes softened. "You're a really good person, Belinda. You care so much about other people. I've never met anyone quite like you. In my heart, I wish I'd been raised in a home like yours. Maybe not having electricity isn't so stinkin' important after all."

Belinda smiled faintly and rose from the bed. "I'll leave now, but I'll see you tomorrow and we'll talk some more—if you want to."

After she left for home, she prayed about the situation, asking God to do something—anything—to have Madison change her mind. And her heart. Hopefully, once she read about the formation of the baby, she'd change them both.

Lancaster County, Pennsylvania

Becky sat on an old quilt on the ground while Wayne took the kitchen towel off of the wicker basket they'd brought with them. His eyes lit up when he spotted cold fried chicken legs covered in plastic wrap. "I love chicken this way. Did you cook it?"

"Jah, last night. I wanted it to be nice and cold today for our picnic. I made the potato salad, too. I hope you like it."

He removed the plastic container with the salad and took off the lid. "Looks gut. You like cooking? That's what you told me."

"I do. I like housekeeping too." She reached over and removed a baggie with homemade pickles and set it down on the quilt. Then she took out paper plates and two plastic forks from the basket and passed one over.

"Nobody likes to clean," he remarked, smiling over at her.

"I do. You can make it fun. I sing while I work."

"I've heard you at the Sings. You have a pretty voice. High."

"Too high. Sometimes I sound squeaky."

"Nee. I never heard you squeak."

"Well, maybe you weren't listening."

"Nee, I always listen to you sing."

"Really?"

"Jah, really. I watch you sometimes when you're with your friends. You always have a smile on your face. I like that about you."

Becky knew her face was probably scarlet by now. She could feel the heat rise in her neck.

"Look," he said reaching in the basket and finding wet paper towels, "you even thought about our messy hands."

Becky laughed. "I've eaten enough fried chicken to know it's sloppy."

"So what did you make for dessert?"

"Just brownies."

"I love your brownies. I hope you brought a lot of them."

Becky nodded. "I'll make you more when they're gone."

They sat and ate, barely speaking for a few minutes. She hoped her tummy wouldn't rumble. She'd been too excited to eat breakfast and she could feel her stomach objecting to the absence of food. Once he looked over with a grin and she wanted to melt into the ground. She was convinced it was because he heard her insides growling. Oh my.

After they finished up, Becky put everything back in the basket and lay back on the quilt to look up at the sky. The sun felt glorious on her face. It had been a long winter and she had hated being cold. She closed her eyes and let out a sigh. Before she reopened them, she felt pressure on her lips. Sweet, gentle pressure. Her eyes popped open and she looked upon Wayne's closed eyes ever so near. My goodness, was this really happening? Next she felt his lips on her cheek and then his hand lifted her kapp off her head.

"Nee, not my kapp."

"I'm sorry. Why not?"

"You know only a woman's husband looks at her hair."

"I wasn't going to take it down. I just didn't want you to get your kapp dirty."

Becky regretted her remark about husbands. He'd think she was presumptuous, for sure. But before she could figure out what to say or do next, he had her hands in his and he was pulling her up to a standing position. Once she was erect, he dropped one of her hands and led her toward the brook beyond the area where they were picnicking. He didn't say a word. Her hand was damp from perspiration, but he didn't seem the least concerned. When they got to the edge of the brook, he turned her toward him and asked if he could kiss her again. She stuttered, "I guess so."

This time she placed her own arms around his back and took in his scent. Clean and masculine. Surely it was a dream and she'd soon awaken. After he kissed her, he released her. "I like you a lot, Becky. I don't know why I never noticed you till lately."

"I don't know either. I was always around."

"I guess I just thought of you as my schwester's friend."

"I have to confess something, Wayne."

"Jah?" His brows arched.

"I've liked you for a long time."

He grinned and stifled a laugh. "Really? Like how long?"

"Since I first saw you."

"Wow! That's really cute. I'm a year younger than you."

"It doesn't matter to me. Does it to you?"

"Nee. Not at all. I like the idea of dating older women. So we can date now, right?"

"I think today was a date."

"Oh, jah, that's for sure. So we can have a second date."

"That sounds gut, but I don't think we should kiss again, do you?"

He tilted his head and gave her a half smile. "I'll try not to, but you never know."

She giggled. "Don't I have anything to say about it?"

"Oh, jah. You can yell at me after I do it."

"Wayne, you're terrible!"

"That's what they all say."

"You've kissed a lot of girls before me, haven't you?"

"Not that many. But, Becky, you have the sweetest lips of all."

Becky held back a giggle. Then her lips drew down as she weighed her next words. "I don't want to be hurt. If you're dating me, will you date other girls at the same time?"

"Nee. Just you, Becky." He took her hand again and they went back to the picnic area. Dark clouds gathered overhead and they decided to pack up before the rains came.

After Wayne dropped her off at her house, she ran indoors just in time to avoid the downpour, but nothing could dampen her spirits. It was without doubt, the best day of her entire life.

Chapter Twenty
Holmes County, Ohio

The next afternoon when Madison returned from school, she beckoned Belinda to follow her into her bedroom. Belinda finished changing Lottie and laid her in the crib for a nap.

Then she went in and found Madison lying on her bed, her arm over her eyes. Belinda sat on the edge and patted her friend on the arm. "You okay?"

"I'll never be okay again. Why did you have me look that stuff up? Good grief, the baby's hands are forming and even the ears and eyes. Can you believe it? I always heard it was nothing much till you felt it kick. Why do people lie to you?"

"I wish I had the answer. It's terrible when you think about it. I bet most girls wouldn't have abortions if they knew the truth."

"I was better off not knowing. It was gonna be easy. Now I don't know if I can do it. I've decided to talk to my father about everything. I actually tried praying last night first."

"Gut. Did it help you with your decision to tell him?"

"Maybe. I don't know, but I really don't want to deal with this alone. It is a major decision. I realize that now."

"When will you tell him?"

"Tonight. Before I chicken out."

"What about Deb?"

"What about her? I don't care what she thinks."

"It's just that your father loves her and he probably wants her thoughts about it."

"Whatever. If she's there, so be it."

"I'm glad you've decided to tell them, Madison. Who knows? Maybe they'll want to raise the baby for you till you're old enough to take care of it yourself."

"I doubt that. Having Lottie was traumatic enough around here. You'd think Deb was the only woman in the world to give birth. She played it to the hilt. My father treated her like she was made of tissue paper. It was disgusting the way he babied her."

"Maybe he'd do the same for you."

"Yeah right. So are you leaving now? I'll watch Lottie when you go."

"I should leave soon. Mamm wants me to help put up asparagus, but if you want to talk…"

"That's okay. Just wish me luck about tonight."

"I'll do better than that. I'll pray for you."

Madison's eyes widened. "Now?"

"Either now or later, whichever way you want it."

"Huh. I guess it would be okay to do it now. Just don't make it too long and boring."

Belinda grinned. "Jah, I'll hurry." They closed their eyes and Belinda kept her hand on Madison's arm as she began.

"Dear God,

Thank you for listening to this prayer. Please help Belinda through her pregnancy and be with her when she talks to her father and maybe step-mother tonight. Don't let them be too mad at her. Also, help Madison to make the right decision and comfort her. Danki, I mean—thank you.

Amen."

Madison looked over with a weak smile. "Thanks, Belinda. I hope He hears you."

"He does. I'm certain of that. I'll run along now. Lottie's probably gonna sleep another half hour or so."

"I'll leave my door open. See you tomorrow."

"Jah. I'm gonna be thinking and praying a lot for you tonight. What time do you think they'll be home?"

"No idea. Usually it's around eight, but you never know. I just hope my dad's in a good mood."

"That would be gut."

Belinda went downstairs and said goodbye to Vera, who was polishing silver in the kitchen.

"What's wrong with our princess lately? She's been even more miserable than normal."

"I…I guess she has things on her mind. We just have to be patient, is all."

"That's easier said than done. She's listening for her sister?"

"Jah. She'll take care of her."

"I'm surprised she's as good with Lottie as she is. Probably your influence."

"I don't know about that, but she does love her, that's for sure."

"Glad somebody does. Her mother hardly looks at her when she comes home. Lottie's father seems more interested in her than she does. He's not a bad sort for a lawyer."

"Lawyers are bad?"

Vera laughed. "It's an Englisher's joke. Don't pay no heed."

"Okay. I'll see you tomorrow, Vera."

Belinda left and walked home. At least Madison had accepted prayer. Even prayed herself. That was a major step in the right direction.

Lancaster County, Pennsylvania

Katie stopped at her parent's home on the way back from school the next day. Mary had told her Sunday that she would have rhubarb harvested for her. Josiah's favorite pie was strawberry-rhubarb so she wanted to surprise him. When she arrived, the family was seated in the kitchen having tea. Oma looked perky in a new dress Mary had sewn for her. She looked younger than she'd looked for months.

"Come sit with us, dochder," Mary said when she saw her come through the doorway. "Tea?"

"Jah, I'll have a cup. I don't have too much time, since I want to get home to make supper, but I'll stay for a few minutes."

"You look real gut, Katie," Leroy said, smiling over at his daughter. "Your color gets better all the time."

"I feel pretty gut. Not like sick at all, though I get tired a little quick."

"Teaching takes a lot out of you," Mary said.

Wayne was relaxing at the end of the table. He had his arms behind his head and his legs were stretched under the table. So far he hadn't said a word.

"Wayne, why are you so silent?" Mary asked her son.

"Just waiting till there's a lull so I can be heard." He grinned at Katie. "So you've been trying to fix me up with your friend for some time now."

"What do you mean?" Katie looked over at Wayne and tried to keep a straight face.

"You know. Becky told me she's liked me for a long time. Now I know why she kept coming by."

"Are you mad?"

Everyone watched for his reaction.

"Nee. I think it's funny, is all. I never even noticed her till lately."

"Ah, but now you do," Leroy said with a crooked smile.

"I guess so. She's pretty cute and has a sweet smile. I like pleasant girls."

"Oh, she is ever so pleasant," Katie said quickly. "I never see her look mean at all."

"Like you'd tell me the truth if you did."

"Wayne, I don't lie. I would tell you. The only time she had a sad face was when she thought you'd never notice her."

Wayne laughed out loud. "Well, I've noticed her now and we're dating just in case anyone's interested."

Mary grinned over at her son. "You could do worse. I like Becky ever so much. In fact, I thought you were sweet on her last year."

Leroy nodded in agreement.

Oma just sat there taking it all in. Then she added, "So when's the wedding going to be?"

The family laughed together. Mary shook her head. "My mudder loves weddings, that's for certain."

"You'll be the first to find out, Oma," Wayne said as he winked across the table at her.

Chapter Twenty-One
Holmes County, Ohio

Madison paced the floor. It was quarter of eight and her parents hadn't arrived home yet. Lottie was due to wake up for a feeding, but Vera had taken over her care since Madison needed a nap earlier. Her nausea had returned and she wondered if it was from stress or the pregnancy. Probably both.

At last, she heard the garage door open from under the living room. It's rumble under her feet caused her to nearly gag as she realized it was now time to address this whole mess with her father. Maybe she'd be lucky and Deb would be too busy to listen in. She didn't need that woman's condemnation.

When they came through the basement door into the hallway, she felt her body stiffen. They stopped at the entrance to the living room when they saw Madison standing there.

"What's going on, Madison," her father, Ken, asked. "You look pale."

"Oh it's probably the lighting."

Deb looked at her too. "You might be coming down with the flu. I hope you didn't hold Lottie."

"I'm not sick, all right?"

Ken shot a glare towards his daughter. "Don't speak to Deb like that. She's just concerned for the baby, you know."

"Right. Listen if you're too busy to talk about something with me, I can wait—"

"Give me a few minutes to change into something more comfortable. Deb, why don't you fix us some martinis? We can relax before we eat something."

"I guess I should check Lottie first. Oh, maybe Vera will keep an eye on her for us. I could sure use a drink. I need to change first, though. I hate these heels."

Madison stood and watched as they both went upstairs. Her heart was beating so rapidly, she thought it might pop out of her chest.

Deb came down first and walked past her into the kitchen to make martinis. It seemed to take forever before her dad appeared on the stairs. Madison stood motionless in the hallway. He looked at her quizzically and then nodded towards the den. "We'll meet you in there, Madison. I hope you don't need more money for clothes. You went way over your budget last month."

"No, it's not about money."

"Let me give Deb a hand."

Before he turned, she spoke up. "Dad, can we talk in private?"

He stared at her and clenched his jaw. "Whatever you have to tell me, you can tell my wife." He walked abruptly away from her towards the kitchen.

Madison made her way into the den and sat on one of the plaid loveseats. She folded her arms and stared straight ahead. She begged silently to God, her new friend, to help her through the next hour.

Her father returned with a tray of cut cheese and crackers, along with a martini pitcher. Deb followed behind with their glasses and set them on the mahogany coffee table. She glanced over at Madison and frowned. "It's been a tough day in court for your father. I hope you're not going to upset him with one of your schemes."

"Schemes? I have no idea what you're talking about."

"All right. Let's try to be civil." He took one of the glasses from Deb's hand and they sat together on a matching love seat across from Madison. Deb poured the liquor into each of their glasses.

"So what's so important that you couldn't wait until the week-end?" Ken asked as he took a chunk of cheese and stuck it in his mouth.

"I'm pregnant."

He began to choke and Deb grabbed a cocktail napkin and held it over his mouth till he was able to collect himself.

"Nothing like being blunt," Deb said, glaring at her step-daughter.

"There wasn't any way to sugar-coat it."

"How in heaven's name did you manage to get yourself pregnant?" Ken asked, his voice level, but angry.

Deb jumped in. "You don't have to ask her that. It's obvious she's aware of the consequences of her promiscuity."

"I only had one boyfriend," she said defensively.

"You're only sixteen, for Pete's sake," Ken said, his eyes dark.

"Well we'll just make an appointment for you to get rid of it before anyone else finds out," Deb said.

"Does the boy know?" her father asked.

"No."

"So who, pray tell, is the lucky father?" Deb asked sarcastically.

"We don't need to know that," Ken said.

"I don't want to get rid of it," Madison said, causing them to both stiffen and then stare at each other.

"You certainly can't take care of an infant," Deb said, as she turned her eyes and fired them into Madison's.

"I can give it up for adoption."

"You'd do that? Go through nine months and give it away?" Her father asked.

"It's better than killing it, isn't it!"

"It's not a baby yet, for heaven's sake," Deb said. "It's merely tissue forming."

"Not true! Everyone lies about it! I looked it up and it's not just tissue! It's way more. It's a little baby already with arms forming and even eyes! Don't lie to me!"

"Madison, stop it right now. Deb knows more about these things than you do."

"No, she doesn't. She's lying to you too, Dad. She just doesn't want the embarrassment of her step-daughter getting pregnant out of wedlock. But this is more than that. I look at Lottie and she's so cute and perfect. God's doing that in my body. He's making a new life!"

"Where did this God stuff come from?" Deb said, clucking her tongue. "You never worried about God before. Maybe if you'd thought before you—"

"Deb, just be quiet," Ken said, creasing his brows together. "Let the girl talk. It is her decision in the end."

"She's too young to make such an important decision. Certainly you don't want her to have this baby, do you?"

"I don't know how I feel. It's my grandchild, you know. Maybe we could raise it."

"Don't be ridiculous. It's bad enough I have Lottie to worry about. My profession has to come first."

"So I noticed," he said, contempt registering in his eyes. Then he turned to Madison. "You would actually want to have the child adopted out?"

She nodded as tears rolled down her face. "I know I'm too young to be a good mother and I don't want to see my child grow up unloved. It would be better to let a couple raise it who really wanted it. Lots of people are looking to adopt. I read that somewhere."

"That's true. That's a very unselfish act of yours, Madison. I have to admit, I'm proud of you."

Deb stood up and raised her arms. "Proud? She comes in admitting she's been tramping around and gets herself pregnant, and you're *proud?* What's come over you? What if they find out at the law firm? You're looking to become a partner. What then?"

"Deb, that has nothing to do with it. I'm sure it wouldn't matter one iota. These things happen. It's not the end of the world. If Madison is willing to go through with this pregnancy, knowing she'd have to give the baby up, then I'm going to support her decision."

"Well, I think it's ridiculous! But then no one seems to care what I think."

"Of course I care, but you don't really have a good reason for her not to carry this child to term. It is a life, you know. I think of Lottie and realize we could have chosen to end her life. What a tragedy that would have been. I don't want Madison to abort and then live with the consequences of that decision her whole life, even if it would be simpler for you."

"Well, I'm not going to pamper her. If she gets sick, it's her problem."

"I never expected you to care for me," Madison said, biting the words. "You never have before. What would be different now?"

"Listen, we have to get through these next months together somehow," her father said. "Let's make it easier on everyone and try to get along. We should be supportive of each other."

"I've always tried to get along," Deb remarked. "It's your daughter who makes life difficult."

"I'm not going to get into who's to blame for what," he said. "Sit down and we'll talk about this calmly."

Deb dropped down onto the loveseat and gulped her drink down.

He went on. "Madison, when is your baby due?"

"I guess around December sometime. I'm not sure."

"Have you seen a doctor?"

"No, but I did a pregnancy test."

"Then tomorrow we'll make an appointment for you. We can talk to the doctor about the adoption thing when we see him. I'll check with my internist, Dr. Guerney, tomorrow. We'll see who he recommends for your obstetrician."

Deb chewed on a cracker and looked straight ahead.

"Thanks for listening to me, Dad. It's funny, I wanted to just go for an abortion, but when I read about the fetus and how it was forming…well, I was just so amazed—all I could think of was Lottie. What if she'd never been born? My heart just changed in an instant. I don't even know how, but all of a sudden I wanted to give my own baby a chance. You know what I mean?" She held her hand over her flat stomach and looked over at her father, her eyes pleading for him to understand.

"I think I understand, honey. What about the father though? Do you think you should talk to him about it? You might need his okay to give it up for adoption."

"No way! He could care less. I know he'd push for an abortion. I don't want him to know anything about this. Knowing him, he'd deny he was the father anyway."

Deb looked up. "Maybe he knows more than we do."

Ken looked at her in anger. "Enough, Deb! I'd prefer you either leave the room or try your best to work with us on this."

"Well, I never!" She rose and stomped out of the room and up the stairs. Madison heard Lottie cry out and then Deb's shrill voice as she made her way into the nursery. "Where's Vera? I'm way too beat to take care of this baby."

Ken looked over at Madison and shrugged. "She's got a headache, I'm afraid."

"No, Dad, she *is* a headache."

"I'll ignore that remark. Are you eating properly?"

"I guess so. I've been throwing up some days, so food doesn't look too inviting at this stage."

146

"I see. So who else knows about this? Does Vera know?"

"No. Only you guys and Belinda."

"The Amish girl?"

"That's the only Belinda I know."

"She must be impressed with your morals."

"Dad, don't rub it in. I know it was wrong. If only I could live it over. Actually, Belinda is really good about it. She's real concerned for me. It was her idea to look it up on the Internet and see how the baby's developing."

"Really."

"And she prayed with me."

"Seriously? So she's a good influence."

"I guess so. I really like her a lot. In fact, she's my best friend at this point. I haven't told any of my other friends about it. I don't want to, but I guess I won't be able to keep it a secret forever."

"Would you want to go visit Aunt Beth in Vermont till the time comes?"

"I hardly know your sister. I'll hang out here, I guess, though I dread it. Most of all, I dread having Deb around all the time."

"If you want to consider it, I can call Beth and find out if it's okay with her."

"No, not yet. Let me think about it some more first. I have time right now. I won't show for a while yet and I want to finish school. I only have two weeks left for the year."

"You could take courses over the next year, I guess."

"Dad, I know you're trying to help me, but I can't think that far ahead. This whole thing has been a nightmare. I need to go one day at a time."

He rose and came over to sit next to her. "Honey," he said as he placed his arm around her shoulders, "we'll get you through this. I'm proud of you for your decision. I'm sorry it happened, but I think you're making the right choice."

"To be honest? I don't even feel I have a choice at this point. I think I'd never forgive myself if I didn't have this baby. If I were older, I'd keep it, but I know I'd be a lousy mother. As much as I love Lottie, I hate it when she cries and I get sick of watching her sometimes. I'd never hurt her, but babysitting just isn't my thing."

"Not at sixteen. Someday, things will be different. Now let's go check out the refrigerator. I'm starving."

They went arm and arm into the kitchen and split a ham sandwich. For the first time in a week, Madison felt hunger pangs. A decision had been made and she felt confident it was the correct one.

Chapter Twenty-Two
Lancaster County, Pennsylvania

Leroy poured cream into his coffee mug and stirred slowly, his eyes concentrating on the hot liquid.

Mary set a plate of freshly made donuts in the center of the table and poured herself a cup of coffee. After she sat down across from her husband, she looked over at him. "Why so quiet?"

"Just thinking, is all."

"About?"

"Well, you know we've talked about selling Oma's farmhouse and just keeping most of the acreage."

"I thought since we rented it out to Happy Yoder's cousin, we'd stopped the idea of selling. At least for now."

"Jah, and I guess that's why the subject hasn't come up lately. Anyway, I've been thinking, since Wayne's getting to an age where he'll be thinking of marriage and moving on, we could let him use the house and land. Our tenant is leaving in the fall sometime anyway. He's going back to Minnesota."

"We'd have to talk to Mamm about it. It's her property and she likes the rent coming in."

"She shouldn't care, after all, she ain't got any expenses. We take care of everything."

"I know. I think she just likes feeling independent. I let her buy her own fabric sometimes just so she'll feel gut about it."

"We can ask her about the farmhouse when she gets up later. It'll be up to her, that's for sure. Wayne could pay her a little every month, just like a mortgage."

Mary sipped her hot coffee. "We'll see. Don't you want a donut? They're still warm."

"They look wonderful-gut. Jah, I'll take two, if you don't mind."

She smiled and moved the plate closer to her husband, who placed a couple on his plate. "Were you surprised to hear about Wayne dating Becky?" he asked.

"Not at all. Those two have flirted together for years. Surely he knew she had a crush on him. He's just enjoying the attention, is all."

"Think it's serious?"

Mary shrugged. "I kind of hope so. I've always liked Becky. She's a sweet girl and I like her whole family. Gut people."

"Jah. Seems so. She and Katie have been friends since they were toddlers."

"And they work well together teaching."

"I feel bad for our Katie, Mary. I know she'd rather be home raising kinner."

Mary sipped her coffee and broke off a small piece of donut. "Jah, well. We have to accept God's plans, whatever they might be."

"I know. It's just kind of too bad she'll probably never have her own boppli."

"At least she's free of her leukemia."

"As of now, thank Gott." He patted her hand.

"Jah. We must pray it continues this way. As long as she's on the medication, she should be okay. Of course she needs to take care of herself so she doesn't get weak."

Leroy nodded. "She's my little boppli. I'm ever so grateful she's okay now. Gott is gut."

"Jah, you can say that again." Mary reached for another piece of donut and smiled over at Leroy. "He was gut enough to bring you into my life."

Leroy patted her hand. "I'm the one who was blessed. You are the finest wife a man could ever ask for. Danki."

Mary felt tears form. She thought back to when she nearly lost him. Oh, my. How would she have survived without the love of her life?

Holmes County, Ohio

"I'm so glad you told your parents," Belinda said as she lifted Lottie from her crib and laid her on the changing table to put fresh diapers on her.

Madison dropped her book bag on the floor and sat on the rocker watching.

"And they're supporting you in your decision to put the baby up for adoption?"

Madison nodded. "I think Dad would actually bring the kid up, but there's no way I'd let the witch have anything to do with my baby. I want it to have two parents to love it."

"There are plenty of people who will want to adopt your child. I already know one who would."

Madison's jaw dropped. "You do?"

"Jah, a gut friend of mine who lives in Pennsylvania just got married, but she shouldn't, and probably can't, have babies of her own. She had leukemia and has to be on strong medication probably forever. It wouldn't be a gut idea to get pregnant since she'd have to stop taking the medicine while she was expecting, or it could damage the baby."

"Oh, wow. That's rough. But she's okay now?"

"Apparently, she'll never be cured. It just lays asleep."

"You mean she's in remission."

"Jah, that's the word."

"Do you think she'd really want to adopt? She's Amish?"

"Jah to both questions."

"I don't know how my father would feel about having his grandkid be Amish. He'd probably be against it."

"Why? To live in an Amish family is wonderful-gut. You've seen how we live. How would you feel about it? After all, you're the mother. You're the one to make that decision, even though I agree, your father should be part of it."

"I can mention it. Belinda, I'd have to meet the couple. I couldn't just hand it over without knowing them."

"You could get to meet them. I bet they'd get a driver and come right to Ohio to meet you if they thought you'd consider them for the adoption. Do you want me to mention it in my next letter?"

"No, it's too soon. Who knows? I may even have a miscarriage or something. Not that I want to exactly, but it's too early to go blabbing about it. Think how disappointed your friend would be if we agreed to everything and then something happened."

"Jah, you're right. No sense building up her hope. At least you know there is someone you could consider." Belinda lifted the smiling Lottie and held her in her arms. "You, little Lottie, are the cutest boppli in the world. Well, next to my nieces and nephews," she added grinning over at Madison.

"If you were married, would you want my baby?"

"Oh, mercy. I never thought of that. I would have trouble saying no, that's for sure. I love boppli. I'm nowhere near being married though—unfortunately."

"So Jeff hasn't been in touch with you at all?"

Belinda sighed. "Nee. He's seeing another girl anyway. Didn't I tell you?"

"Yeah, you did. That stinks. Guys are so fickle."

"I never thought Jeff was, but I couldn't have meant too much to him or he would still be in the picture. I wish I could get over him."

"That Zeke guy. Any interest at all?"

"I don't know. He's nice enough, but I still love Jeff. I probably always will." She glanced at the clock. "I guess I should leave soon. I promised Zeke I'd go to a frolic with him tonight. I don't really care about it, but I have to get out with people sometimes. I can't just work and sleep."

"I know that feeling. I don't know what I'll do now. I can go out, but I don't feel like it, to tell the truth. Everyone seems so immature. Like they worry about stupid stuff like what color lipstick to buy or when a movie is coming out. I can't relate anymore. Actually, I feel closer to you, Belinda, than to my other friends."

"I'm glad I can be here for you. You're one of my best friends now too. My one friend, Zeke's sister, is planning to stay in Florida. She went down to help a relative and now she loves it there. She's even met an Amish guy she likes, so since most of my friends are married or getting married, it leaves me pretty much alone. Except for my family, of course. So I'm never really alone. We have a ton of relatives."

"Here, I'll take Lottie downstairs so you can leave. Maybe I'll take her out and get some sunshine."

"See you Monday then. I hope you have a gut week-end."

"Right. I wish Deb worked seven days a week."

Belinda laughed. "Maybe she'll change her attitude."

"Fat chance of that. I have no idea what my father saw in her. Oh, well, that's not my problem."

"Hopefully, he doesn't see it as a problem."

They walked down the stairs together and Madison walked as far as the end of the drive with her friend. After Belinda left, Madison contemplated her child being raised by Amish people. Funny, it never would have occurred to her before meeting Belinda, but now it seemed like a good option. Time would tell.

Chapter Twenty-Three
Lancaster County, Pennsylvania

It was the last day of school before summer break. The children were nearly uncontrollable. They were so excited, that Katie and Becky decided to just stay outdoors and let them play field games. Tag and *eck* ball, which was a variation of dodge ball, were two of the boys' favorites.

On the side of the schoolhouse, a group of girls played jump rope, adding songs to their skill.

The teachers sat on folding chairs and watched, occasionally breaking up the inevitable quarrels.

"I am so ready for a break, you can't believe it," Becky remarked as she moved her head quickly to avoid being hit by a soccer ball inadvertently kicked their way.

"Jah, I'm tired, too," Katie added. "There's so much to do at home now. Josiah's busy planting. I'm glad my bruders offered to help out, as well as Josiah's own family. Of course, he helped them several days last week at their farms."

"It works out gut. Everyone helps each other out. That's one thing I love about being Amish."

Katie nodded. "When are you and Wayne going on a date again?"

"This Saturday we're going to go into Lancaster by driver. Just to walk around and see things. Nothing special. I guess we'll have lunch out."

"Sounds like fun. I don't think he's ever done that with another girl, Beck. Maybe it means something."

"I have to tell you a secret. But you can't let anyone else hear."

Katie grinned as she leaned closer. Becky was taking no chance on anyone hearing her. She whispered. "Your bruder kissed me. More than once, too."

"Oh, dear. Were you mad?"

"Katie, it was wonderful-gut! Why would I be mad?"

"He hasn't asked you to marry him yet, has he?"

"Nee, but I think it's coming soon. I just have a feeling. I didn't want to hurt him." She twisted her kapp ribbon and tilted her head.

"Wayne moves quickly, I'm afraid." Katie remarked, fearful her friend was getting too serious, too quickly.

"I told him no more kissing."

"And you believe he won't try again?"

Becky sighed and leaned back against the chair. "I hope he does."

Katie giggled. "You are something else."

"Well, didn't Josiah kiss you?"

"Jah, but we were engaged. I think."

"Anyway, don't tell a soul. We won't have an opportunity in Lancaster, so I'm safe."

"Please be careful not to fall too hard for him. There's no guarantee that he's serious, Becky."

"You don't think he likes me?" Her brows creased.

"Nee, I do! Really! But he's liked girls before and then broken off. I just don't want you to get hurt."

"I'll be careful. It's too late to hold back my feelings. I won't tell him I love him, but I can't pretend I'd get over it fast if he broke off."

"I just hope it works out for you. I'd love to have you as a sister-in-law. How neat that would be."

"And our kids could play together…Oh, Katie, I'm sorry. I totally forgot."

Katie swallowed hard and forced a smile. "It's okay. Really. Besides, no one knows the future."

"That's true. Uh-oh, another dispute between Orville and Mose," Becky said as loud voices disturbed their conversation. "We'd better break it up."

"You can't believe how relieved I am that we'll be done teaching," Katie said, rising. The girls walked over to the two hot-heads and separated them.

At last it was time to dismiss everyone for the summer. Some of the girls came over for hugs and then a couple buggies showed up to take some of the students home. The rest of the young scholars took off by foot or scooter. Once everyone had left, Katie and Becky finished cleaning the school room and left. They made plans to return in a week to straighten out the papers and supplies, though the school board paid a woman to do the heavy cleaning before school began again in the fall. Volunteers helped out, too.

Katie took a nap when she got home. Josiah had hitched four of his sturdiest work horses to a plow. He waved at her, but kept working. The weather forecast predicted heavy rains for the next several days. Maybe they'd have some special time together if he couldn't work outside. She could use some fun time with her husband. There was an underlying depression that followed her around all the time now and even prayer didn't seem to alleviate it entirely, though it helped. If only.

Holmes County, Ohio

Belinda was lonelier over the week-ends, though she and her family stayed busy the whole time. She and her mother, Grace, along with Nellie went over to the Hershberger's on Saturday to help them prepare for the Sunday service, which would be held in their barn the following day. Several other neighbors showed up to help out. Belinda saw Zeke arrive with two of his brothers. He came right over to her.

"Hallo, Belinda. It's nice of you to help out."

"That's what we do, ain't it?" she said smiling back. "Help our neighbors?"

"Jah, you're right about that. I was gonna stop over to see you later on my way home. Do you want to go fishing with me?"

"I hate to fish."

"You can watch."

"That would be boring, I'm afraid," she said as she walked towards the kitchen door from the porch, which she had been sweeping.

"I don't have to go fishing then. Maybe we can just go for a walk."

"Maybe."

His face lit up like a fireworks display. "I'll go get the seats set up then and my bruders can find another way home so we can use my buggy."

"I'll be awhile, Zeke. There's a lot to do yet, I'm thinking."

"Whenever you're ready, just let me know." He walked away with quick strides. He seemed two inches taller. Belinda watched and smiled to herself. Okay, so she wasn't in love with him, but he was a nice Amishman and he found her attractive. That had to count for something. As long as it remained platonic on both their parts, what was the harm?

The way things looked now, Jeff was out of her life anyway. Perhaps it was just as well. Even turning Mennonite seemed like too much to ask now. Her mother had spoken to her about taking her kneeling vows soon. She still hesitated to take that final step to enter the church. After that, there would be no turning back. Something continued to nag at her heart. She did not feel free to move in that direction. Not yet.

The women chatted as they wiped off the dishes and folded paper napkins. It was fun to hear about the latest news in the community. Grace took notes of those who needed get well cards or meals and Belinda talked with two of her friends who were recently married. They were both pregnant and she felt out of touch, though she told them about Lottie and her cute antics. They smiled and nodded, but then resumed their discussion of their pregnancies. Belinda walked away and joined Nellie who was washing down the counters. She took a dishtowel and dried them.

"I saw you talking to Zeke," Nellie said, grinning at her big sister.

"Jah. That's all we do, Nellie. We just talk. Don't get any ideas."

"He likes you. I can tell. Don't hurt him, Belinda. He's a nice guy."

"I'm just friends with him. You know that."

"His brudder said he's in love with you."

"Oh, no. Goodness sakes, we hardly know each other."

"You used to play *Crockenole* with him. Remember?"

"That was ages ago. I played with tons of people."

"Well, don't let him get too personal with you if you still like Jeff. It wouldn't be fair."

"Nellie. Nellie. You sound like Mamm. You take care of your own problems."

"Don't look now, but he's coming up behind you."

Zeke stopped when he was a few feet away and Belinda turned towards him. "Are you done, Belinda?" he asked.

"She can be. I'll take over," Nellie said. Belinda turned and scowled at Nellie behind his back. Nellie forced back a grin and reached for the dishtowel in Belinda's hand. "Go. I'll tell Mamm."

"Danki, Nellie. That's nice of you," Zeke said as he twisted the rim of his hat, which he held in front of him.

"I guess I can leave then," she said as she looked over at her friends who were still engrossed in their conversation. Nellie went over to tell their mamm and

Grace nodded over at Belinda and Zeke, a wide smile forming as she waved.

Zeke held out his hand and helped Belinda step up into the open buggy and then took his place in the driver's seat and reached for the reins. Clicking his tongue and pulling slightly on the reins, his horse backed up and headed up the drive to the road. The horse clopped along rhythmically and Zeke waved to friends going the opposite direction.

He asked Belinda about her baby-sitting job and she told him all about Lottie's accomplishments. "She sits up almost by herself now. And she just popped another tooth."

"You want a large family?" he asked as he kept his eyes straight ahead.

"Oh, jah. Probably at least six. Maybe ten. Who knows?"

"I guess your English friend wasn't so keen on so many kinner, was he?"

She looked over and noted his jaw was firm and his lips thin. "I don't want to talk about him."

He glanced over and relaxed his jaw slightly. "Sorry. I shouldn't have said that. It is over though, right?"

"I don't see him anymore, if that's what you mean," she answered, looking down at her apron, water-spotted from washing pots earlier. She traced a wide stain with her finger.

"Is that the way you want it?"

"That's the way it is. Want it or not."

"Be honest, Belinda. Are you over him yet?" She saw him turn his gaze her way.

She looked into his eyes. He had a right to know, didn't he? "I'm not sure I'll ever be over him, Zeke. You need to know that, I guess."

He returned his eyes to the road ahead and hastened the speed of his horse. They were silent for several minutes until Belinda remarked about a deer she saw in an open field.

Zeke glanced over and nodded. Finally he pulled over to a grassy area and reined in his horse. "We can take a trail here. I've walked it before and it's only about a mile."

"Jah? Okay. My feet are a bit tired, so a mile is about all I can do right now." Belinda was used to being on her feet most of every day. Would he even believe her excuse?

After tethering the horse to a tree, they walked slowly down a trodden path, Belinda walking ahead of Zeke to set the pace. They went through a woodsy area and then came to open fields. "This property belongs to a cousin of mine," he mentioned when they stopped to view the pasture.

"It's pretty here," she said as she surveyed the vista. Cows were grazing across the open pasture intermingled with a few sheep. The temperature had risen into the low eighties.

Zeke took several steps, leaned against a large maple tree and folded his arms. "I may as well tell you what's on my mind, Belinda. It has been for quite some time now."

She looked over at him. His expression was somber and she dreaded hearing his words. She had never meant to lead him on. Surely he wasn't…

"I know you don't love me," he continued, "but that's not always that important. Love can follow. I guess what I'm trying to say is, I'd like you to be my wife even though I know you don't love me yet. I think I love you enough for both of us. I have for a long time now. You're the only girl I've ever really cared about."

"Don't, Zeke. Please don't continue. I'm sorry if you think I've lead you on in any way—"

"Nee, you've been honest with me. But Belinda, you know down deep that you need an Amish husband. You're Amish through and through. I've watched you and I know you couldn't be happy away from your people. I'm offering you a home and a life you would be familiar with. That Jeff guy couldn't care that much or he'd turn Amish for you."

"It's not that easy a thing to do, Zeke. You know better than that. I wouldn't want a man to change his religion just for me. It wouldn't be honest."

"Did he want you to change for him?"

"It's not your concern what he wanted. I'm sorry, I don't mean to sound angry," she added after analyzing the tone she'd used. "What Jeff and I felt for each other is not anyone's business. It's over and I'm dealing with it. It just takes time."

"Maybe I should have waited then. Look, Belinda, take your time. As much as you need, but know I'll be waiting for an answer. I won't bring it up again, I promise. Just be fair to me and if you make a definite decision, let me be the first to hear. Is that reasonable?"

"That's more than fair, Zeke. Danki for understanding. You are a really nice person and I'm honored that you love me. If I could just make myself feel things I would make myself love you as well, but it's not that easy."

He nodded and looked down at the ground, shoving some loose soil with his foot. "So now you know. If you decide to marry me, you need to take your vows before winter so we can marry in January or February."

"I'm afraid you're pushing me now, Zeke. You said you'd—"

He smiled and shook his head. "I guess you're right. Okay. Let's just finish our walk and I'll try to behave."

When he dropped Belinda off at her home, she went up to her room and flopped on her bed and wept. If only she could make herself love him. All her problems would be solved. If only.

Chapter Twenty-Four
Holmes County, Ohio

Jeff laid his half-eaten burger on the paper plate and looked over at Carrie who was carrying on a conversation with Randy. She almost looked Mennonite now that she'd turned to wearing skirts to church and looser blouses. Of course, she left her head uncovered, but there were several other young women who had not resorted to using the familiar crinoline coverings. At least she didn't look sensuous now. Randy seemed totally enamored of his sister and she now attended church at the meeting house weekly with him.

Megan sat on Jeff's right and turned from her discussion with her friend to observe him. He looked over and smiled.

"You seem awfully quiet today," she mentioned. "You feel okay?"

"I'm fine, I guess."

"Working too hard?" She smiled and her cheek dimpled. He felt his heart quicken. Was he actually forgetting his feelings for Belinda? A combination of guilt and confusion made him uneasy. Why was he vacillating?

"It's been a busy week. At least I'm done with studying for the summer, but we've been knocking ourselves out landscaping."

"You still love it though, right?"

"I guess."

Megan inserted a potato chip in her mouth and tilted her head. "Are you questioning your career goals, Jeff?"

"I'm questioning everything in my life at the moment."

Her eyes left his and she concentrated on her chips. "Everything, and everyone?"

"Oh, Megan. I don't know what's wrong with me. Forgive me if I'm boring you."

She laughed lightly and pushed her plate to the side. "You can talk to me. I hope you know I'm a good friend."

He placed his hand next to hers and touched it with his forefinger. "I know and I'm grateful. Maybe we can leave the others and go for a spin."

They excused themselves and drove through the countryside. When they got to one of the recreational parks in the area, he parked his car and they walked side-by-side around the tennis courts. "Do you play tennis, Jeff?" she asked.

"Sometimes. I'm not very proficient at it."

"We should play together sometime. I'm not good either, but it's still excellent exercise."

"Yeah."

"Unless you'd rather not," she added, sneaking a peek at his expression.

"No, that would be fine." His mouth remained turned down.

"Look, Jeff, let's be truthful with each other. I don't want to get involved with you if you're still holding out for Belinda. I'm afraid I'm starting to care about you too much."

He stopped and turned towards her. They looked intently into each other's eyes. Then Jeff broke the silence. "You're a lovely girl. I really like you a lot, Megan. I wish I could tell you it was totally over between Belinda and me, but I'd be lying. You know I've been seeing an Amish guy almost every week who's been telling me about the *Ordnung* and all the ways of the Amish. I'm still considering the change now that I realize Belinda can't—or won't—leave her community. I just have to be sure in my heart I can do it and that I want to do it."

"It's hard for me to understand her not leaving for the Mennonite religion. It's so close except for the few areas, which don't seem that important to me. Electricity and cars are just things, not moral issues, as far as I can see."

"My friend, Horace, agrees on the one hand, but then explains why it could be just a slippery slope. You give in here and then pretty soon you're bending the rules for everyone. He's afraid in time, you'd lose the closeness of the community and eventually the young would abandon their other beliefs. He has a point."

She nodded. "I guess so. I still see my family, but you're right. Things aren't the same and never will be, I'm afraid. Maybe we shouldn't spend time alone together, Jeff, at least until you sort out your feelings. I've already been hurt in one relationship."

"Really? Anyone I know?"

"No. He was Amish. I thought he really loved me, but then he started seeing my best friend on the side and before you knew it, they were engaged to marry."

"Is that one reason you left the Amish?"

She took a few steps and sat on a wooden bench. "Maybe. Lots of factors entered into it. Anyway, I don't want to be hurt again."

"You've been up-front with me, Megan, so let me be honest with you. I can't let myself feel anything stronger than friendship with you or anyone else yet. Not until I know that things are finished between Belinda and me. If it's definitely over, I know I'd want to spend more time with you. You're very special and I do feel more than an attraction already. It's just hard to let myself go. I hope you understand."

She reached up and wiped her eye with her sleeve and nodded, without looking directly at him. "Let's leave it at that then, Jeff. We can still see each other when we're with others, but no more time alone. Okay?"

He nodded and then placed his hands on her upper arms. "You're so sweet. I hope I'm not making a huge mistake." Then he leaned over and kissed her forehead. "Thanks for trying to understand me."

She stood and moved away, heading for the car. They didn't converse anymore and he drove her to her home. She climbed out and smiled slightly. "See you, Jeff."

"See you, Megan."

He drove off slowly without glancing back. Was he a fool? Was it indeed over with Belinda? His heart ached as he made a decision. He'd have to see her at least once more before allowing his heart to lean towards another, but not yet. Too many decisions needed to be made. His indecisiveness was killing him.

He checked his watch. Maybe Horace could help him. He headed over to the Amish farm.

Lancaster County, Pennsylvania

Mary looked out her kitchen window. Leroy and Wayne were cutting down their first hay of the season. With rain forecasted, they worked feverishly to finish the job.

It was early July and the temperatures were climbing swiftly. Mary turned off the water after filling the tea kettle and set it on the stove to heat. She heard buggy wheels on the drive and looked out to see Katie arrive. Mary smiled as she took down Katie's favorite mug—one shaped like a cow—and placed it next to her own. She watched as her daughter secured her horse and made her way to the kitchen door. When she arrived, they hugged each other. Oma came into the room when she heard their voices, and Mary reached for a third mug. After perfunctory remarks, they sat at the table together and drank their tea along with fresh biscuits.

Katie stirred sugar into her mug and then looked up at her mother and grandmother. "I have some news, I think, but I don't want you to let it get any further than right here in this kitchen."

Oma's brows rose and she set her mug back on the table. Mary, too, stopped sipping and looked over at her daughter. "Jah? Gut news or bad?"

"I guess really gut. I think I'm in a family way."

Oma grinned and nodded in response, but Mary just allowed her jaw to drop. "You think it or you know it?" she asked.

"Well, I'm more than three weeks late."

"Maybe it's your medicine throwing you off," Mary suggested.

"Nee, there's more. I don't feel real gut in the mornings and I almost lost my breakfast yesterday. Also my breasts are sore."

"Oh, jah, you're expecting, that's for sure," Oma said nodding.

"I think you should see the midwife, Katie," Mary said. "She can do a test. Does Josiah know?"

Katie shook her head. "I'm almost afraid to tell him. He's worried about me getting my leukemia back if I go off the medicine. Truth is, I'm already off it. When I was two weeks late, I figured I'd better stop taking it. I wouldn't want to harm the boppli."

Mary reached across the table and placed her hand on Katie's. "I don't know whether to be happy or not, Katie. Maybe I'm a bit scared, too."

Katie's eyes filled. "I wanted so much to have my own boppli and yet now that it might be so, I'm nervous too. I'm even afraid to talk to Josiah about it. I hope he won't be upset with me."

"Mercy, what man doesn't want his own kinner?" Oma said.

"Mamm, it's more complicated than that. You know the problems Katie faces. Josiah wants children, but he wants a healthy wife, too."

"The gut Lord is in control, Mary. Leave it in His hands."

"Mamm, I know that. We all do, but sometimes bad things can happen. Gott allows bad things to happen to gut people."

"Don't tell Daed," Katie said to her mother. "It's too early and besides, I know he'll worry the whole time so why tell him now."

"Nee, I won't. We'll wait until everything is for sure. Sometimes things happen early in pregnancy."

"I hope I don't let it slip," Oma said as she clucked her tongue. "I sometimes forget what's a secret and what ain't."

Katie smiled over at her grandmother. "This is one you have to keep, Oma."

"Do you want more tea?" Mary asked her daughter.

"Jah. Sure. I thought I'd be so excited and here I am being all jittery about it. What's wrong with me?"

"It's to be expected, Katie. It ain't the normal thing, I'm sorry to say, though we will pray every single day for a healthy boppli as well as for your own health. After all, if it was real dangerous, your doctor would have been more forceful about suggesting you not get in the family way, right?"

Katie nodded. "I guess you're right. I'm glad I'm not teaching right now though. I'm feeling tired a lot of the time and I lie down sometimes in the afternoon, even more than normal."

"Honey, we can make meals for you," Mary suggested.

"Nee, it gives me something to do. The house stays pretty clean with just the two of us."

Oma looked startled. "Oh, my, I'll need to get started on a baby quilt!"

Mary shook her head. "Mamm, not yet. Remember, it's a secret."

"Oh, shaw, I forgot. Just give me at least three months notice, Katie. I'm not as fast as I used to be."

Katie laughed and patted her grandmother on her arm. "I'll be sure to give you plenty of time, Oma. Danki. I'm going to leave soon. I want to stop by Ruthie's place and pick up some of last year's onions. Mine rooted and we set them in the garden. I need a couple for soup tonight."

"Katie, did your mamm tell you I cooked my own supper last night?" Oma asked proudly.

"Well gut for you, Oma. What did you make?"

"Salad."

"And?"

"Just salad. It was very filling though. I had fresh asparagus cooked and cut-up in it."

"Sounds just fine," Katie said.

"Oh, and your mudder brought in a piece of her fresh spice cake for me. I forgot that part."

Katie laughed. "Any left?" she asked turning toward her mother.

Mary smiled. "Jah, sure. I'll send some home for you and Josiah. I know he loves it."

"When should I tell him about..."

"Probably soon, Katie. Men kind of guess before we even tell them."

"Say a prayer for me then tonight. I think I'll break it to him after supper—if the timing seems right."

"And let us know soon how he took the news. Remember, be patient with him. He may not be happy at first because of your circumstances, but that will change as time goes on. That's for sure."

After a few more minutes chatting, Katie rose to leave. She placed her mug in the sink and turned to hug her mother.

"Try not to worry, dochder," Mary said.

Katie nodded and went over to Oma and kissed the top of her head. Oma smiled up at her. "I kinda hope for a little *maed* this time. I think girls are easier on their mudders."

Katie smiled. "Whatever the gut Lord provides, Oma. I'll be just fine with it."

As Katie headed out towards the road, Oma got up from the table and decided to redd up her rooms.

After she left, Mary sighed and sat back at the table. She placed a bowl of fresh beans before her, to prepare for supper. Her dear Katie looked so fragile. *Lord, please take care of my dochder and the boppli she's carrying. Please don't let anything happen bad to either of them.*

She wiped a tear and reached for the paring knife. At least it was now in God's hands—where it belonged.

Chapter Twenty-Five
Holmes County, Ohio

Belinda was surprised she kept her job baby-sitting once school was out and Madison was unemployed. Her hours were reduced however, and she was usually home by three o'clock, which gave her time to help her mother around the yard and house. Now that it was July, her father and brother were outside nearly all day.

One Friday she and Madison took Lottie to a country club the family belonged to, where they let her enjoy time in the baby pool. At seven months of age, she was a delightful baby and entertained her watchful sitters as she splashed with all her might, giving off a hearty belly laugh as Madison and Belinda pretended to be surprised at being dampened. After a couple hours of playtime, she fell asleep in Belinda's arms while she gave her a bottle. They sat under a shade tree off to the side of the pool and Madison laid back and closed her eyes. "I'm sick of being pregnant already. I don't know how I'll make it to February."

"You hardly show at all. You just look a tiny bit chunky around the waist," Belinda remarked.

"Thanks. Just what I needed to hear. I spotted one of my friends from school. I hope she didn't notice me."

"None of your friends know you're expecting?"

She shook her head. "Why should I give them something to gossip about? I might go stay with my aunt who lives out of state when I get larger. I'm thinking about it anyway."

"Does your father want you to leave?"

"I don't think he cares, but Deb would be absolutely thrilled. That's one reason I'm holding off."

Belinda giggled. "You're funny."

"I mean it. I can't stand to be around her. She barely talks to me anymore."

"That's a shame. She really should try to be kinder." Lottie squirmed, but settled back into Belinda's arms, her pink lips smacking in sucking motions.

"Aren't you hot with her on top of you like that?" Madison asked.

"A little, but she looks so comfortable, I hate to put her down in the carrier."

"See? I wouldn't have the patience. She'd be down instantly. I'd make a lousy mother."

"Don't be so hard on yourself. You're just young. When you're older, you'll change your feelings."

"Maybe. Actually, I hope so. Most guys want a family, even if it's only one kid. Uh, oh, here comes Paisley."

Nothing much happened when she came over. It was obvious she didn't suspect anything wrong about Madison, who had a large beach towel thrown over her whole body and barely looked up as Paisley talked. Her friend seemed uncomfortable around Belinda and spoke directly to Madison about the latest information concerning their mutual friends. After she left, Madison let out a long breath. "She's so lucky. Sometimes I wonder why I let you talk me out of...you know."

"Listen, I just wanted you to take your time with your decision and know all the facts. I didn't make your decision for you."

"I know. Do you think it's safe enough now to write to your Amish friend who has the cancer?"

"I'll leave that up to you. I haven't said a word yet."

"Well, maybe we'll give it another couple months. Probably better that way."

Lottie woke up and pulled herself up to a sitting position. She grinned her toothy smile at the girls and made sweet cooing sounds. Madison smiled and reached over and touched her sister on the cheek. "I wonder if I'm having a girl."

"Are you going to get an ultrasound?"

"Yeah. Soon. I'm sort of scared."

"Why?"

"I don't want to think of it so much as a real baby. I guess it makes me too sad."

"Oh, Madison, it would be so difficult. You're very brave to go through with it, knowing you'll give the baby up for adoption. I really respect you for that."

"It's about the only good decision I've made lately. I should have seen that guy for who he was. Oh, well, too late now. Hey, I pray now, almost every night."

"Gut for you," Belinda said.

"It felt strange at first, like no one was listening, but I did it anyway and you know what? I like the feeling I get. Like maybe God is listening and loves me and all. You could be right."

"I know He's pleased with your decision to give birth, Madison."

"Not too pleased with how it happened, I bet."

"Mmm. Probably not," Belinda said, cocking her head to the side. "You know it can all be wiped clean. All the sin in your life."

"Oh, right. Just like that. 'Sorry God.' 'Oh, that's okay. Just don't do it again, okay?' 'Yeah God, it was a slip-up.'"

"Listen, Madison, maybe it's not just like that, but if you're truly sorry and aware of how you've hurt the Holy Spirit—"

"Who?"

"The Holy Spirit is part of God— Oh, it's hard to explain everything at once. What you need to know is this. God loves you, but he can't look upon sin. He's too holy and perfect, but he wants us to be part of his kingdom and dwell with him when we pass on to the next world. So He made a way."

"Yeah? How?"

"By allowing his son, Jesus Christ, to take all sin on himself."

"Wait, you said once Jesus was perfect. He didn't have sin, right?"

"Right. He was totally sinless. They call him the Lamb of God, but He willingly died on the cross to make a way for us. That's how much He loves us."

"If that's true, that's pretty awesome. I've seen pictures of the cross and all and it looked horrible. Do you think it really happened?"

"Absolutely. There were many witnesses, both to the crucifixion and to the resurrection."

"When he came alive again?"

"Yah."

"What would he want with me then? I'm so stinkin' imperfect."

"We're all sinners, Madison."

"Not you, Belinda. I don't believe that."

Belinda laughed. "Oh, yah, especially me. I've lied, disrespected my parents, gossiped with my friends—"

"Like, who hasn't? That's not a sin."

"Anything that offends God is a sin. And if you break one commandment, it's like you've broken all of them in His eyes."

"Whoa. Tough to be perfect."

"Nee. Impossible and that's why Christ died for us."

"And that's it? We can go on sinning?"

Belinda smiled as she placed her free arm over her heart. "Nee. First you have to really feel sorry here in your heart and realize your sins. Then you need to get right with God. Confess your sins and repent."

"I've seen those signs by those wacko's about repenting."

"They aren't wacko's, but they feel very strongly and sometimes I don't think they go about it the right way, but I don't want to criticize people for their beliefs."

"So let me get this straight. If I think about all the things I've done that were wrong and pray about them and ask God to forgive me, then I'll go to heaven?"

"That's pretty much the way it is. You have to live differently though, if you really make that confession. It's not a joke."

"I wasn't laughing."

"Sorry, I—"

"Kidding Belinda. No, I'm really trying to understand all this. It's a lot to absorb at one time. I'll have to think about it for awhile before I do anything much."

"I understand. Yah, pray about it too, and ask God to help you understand. It's still hard for me to fathom His amazing love for us."

Lottie began to fuss and they decided to head for home. Madison was quiet all the way back to the house. When she drew the car up to the garage she turned toward Belinda. "Thanks for explaining all that stuff. I appreciate your caring, even if I don't believe it all yet."

"I hope you'll give it real thought, Madison. It's even a more important decision than the one you made about the baby. It's an eternal decision."

"Wow! Awesome! So let's get some ice cream."

They went in and relaxed together as they watched Lottie lie on her blanket in the family room and grab the hanging toys on the swing above her.

That night, Madison spent extra time in prayer. If it wasn't true, well, it wouldn't matter much, but if it were true, she wanted to be part of His gift. She needed to be sure and what better way than going to God and talking to Him about her decision.

Chapter Twenty-Six
Lancaster County, Pennsylvania

Josiah carried the trash out to the burn barrel and checked the animals for the last time before retiring for the evening. Katie watched through the window as he came from the barn. Now was as good a time as ever to talk to him. He'd been in an exceptionally pleasant mood all evening. Sometimes he was too tired to discuss anything important. She knew she should take advantage of the moment.

When he came in, he suggested playing "Settlers of Catan," which was one of Katie's favorite board games.

"Jah, I'd like that, but first we should sit and talk a little."

He gave her a puzzled look, but settled down on the sofa next to her. "You're scaring me, Katie. Did something happen to you?"

"In a way, but it's a gut thing, I'm thinking."

"Jah? So tell me."

"I think I'm in a family way." His silence struck her like a bolt of lightening. She nearly feared looking over at him. At last she heard him release a long breath.

"Honey, that's wonderful-gut, ain't it?"

She let out a giggle—relieved at his reaction, though his words were spoken with a tone of caution. "I think so, don't you?"

He drew her closer with his arm and kissed the side of her cheek. "If my Katie is pleased, then so am I. I'm just concerned for you, honey, you know that."

"I know, Josiah. I was almost afraid to tell you."

"Don't be silly. It takes two, you know."

"Oh, jah," she said with a grin. "I'm aware of that."

"So when will you have our boppli? You don't look it, you know."

"I'm only about three weeks late. I figured sometime in February.'

"Whoa. That's a long time away. Do you feel okay?"

"Not great. Lots of nausea in the morning."

"I thought you looked green the other day. My poor Katie-girl. Why didn't you tell me sooner?"

"I wanted to be sure."

"And your medicine?"

"I stopped taking it two weeks ago. I couldn't take a chance."

He nodded. "You have to tell your doctor."

"I have an appointment in two days, remember? I'll tell him then."

Josiah turned her chin towards him and lowered his lips to hers. He kissed her tenderly. "You will be a wonderful mamm."

"Are you upset with me?"

"Nee, of course not. You're very brave, Katie. I just pray Gott will take gut care of you and our little boppli."

"Do you want a son first?"

He touched her cheek with his hand and smiled into her eyes. "It doesn't matter one bit. I just want a healthy boppli as well as a healthy wife."

"You'll be a gut *vatter*, I'm sure of that," Katie added. "I'm so excited now. Maybe I'll have twins like Emma. That would be ever so nice."

"Jah, two for the price of one." He smiled widely and snuggled closer. "Does anyone else know?"

"I told my mamm and grossmammi, but they have to keep it secret for now."

"Was your mamm upset with me?"

"Of course not. Nee, she's concerned, but excited, too. And Oma, she can't wait to start a quilt for the boppli."

Josiah laughed. "She's such a sweet lady. What color will she choose? Oh, and maybe she should do two, just in case."

"I think green and yellow, like the last one she made for Hannah. I won't mention even the possibility of twins. She'd be thrown into a tizzy if she had to make two." Katie laughed at the thought.

"You should go to bed now, Katie. It's almost eight."

"Honey, I'm not sick, just pregnant."

"Jah, but you need to take extra care of yourself."

"How about you? Are you ready for bed?"

"Maybe. I'll come in and hold you anyway till you fall asleep. I want to be near you, especially now."

"My protector. How grateful I am to Gott that He brought us together."

"Jah, and now He's blessing us with a child born of our love. We must thank him tonight before we sleep."

"Jah, tonight and every night. I feel so blessed."

They went up hand-in-hand and Katie fell asleep halfway through her prayer. She dreamt of angels and a tiny cupid—just like the little one forming in her womb.

Holmes County, Ohio

Belinda and Madison walked around the yard with Lottie in the stroller one day in early August. The area was suffering from a three-week drought. Most of the grass was still green, but there were patches of straw-yellow where the lawn was in direct sun.

"I got a letter from my friend today," Belinda said.

"Which friend? The one we hope will adopt my baby?"

"Jah. Katie. She had some news for me. It may make a difference to the adoption idea."

"I bet she's pregnant, right?"

Belinda let out a sigh. "Yah, she's almost three months along. She's only now telling a few people."

"I knew it. It was too good to be true. Now what?"

"There are many couples who want to adopt. Didn't your dad mention he'd talked to someone about it?"

"Nothing came of it."

"Had you told him about Katie?"

"Kind of. When I said she was Amish, he threw a fit."

"Really? Are we so terrible?" Belinda knew she shouldn't allow anger into her heart, but she felt offended. She prayed an instant prayer for forgiveness.

"He's all about success and money and stuff. Just like his witch."

"Did she hear you mention your idea of placing the baby with an Amish family?"

"She heard. All she did was laugh. Like, what's so funny?"

"Would you go against their wishes? I could still ask Katie. She might consider adopting anyway. She loves kinner."

"I'd love to go against Deb's wishes, but I don't know about Dad. I don't want to upset him anymore than he is, but it is my baby, after all. I think if your friend was willing to adopt, I'd broach the subject again. Of course, I haven't met her yet, so I'd have to check her and her husband out first. You understand, don't you?"

"Jah, of course. I'll write back and ask her about it. At least we'd find out if she'd be willing."

"Okay. Write. It doesn't hurt to ask. The more I think about her being raised Amish, the better it feels."

"Do you like knowing that you're carrying a girl?"

"I think it makes it harder, actually. I picture another Lottie sometimes and I get a pit in my stomach at the thought of giving her away, maybe to a stranger. Yet, I can't see myself mothering a kid. I know I'd be lousy."

"What you're doing is very unselfish. Don't forget that."

"Why do I feel so guilty then?"

"I can understand it, but you have to give those guilt feelings up."

"Hey, I pray about it now and it's not quite as bad as it was."

"Have you thought anymore about our discussion about Christ and his plan of salvation?"

"Yeah. I think about it but I'm not sure of anything yet. I picked up a Bible the other day and tried to read it. It didn't make a lot of sense."

"Stick with the New Testament in the beginning. It's easier and it's all about Christ."

"Maybe I'll try that. I read part of the first book, Genesis. It was wild."

Belinda laughed and Lottie looked up and grinned. Then she went back to chewing her cloth bunny.

"Some of it is hard, but it's all true, Madison."

"Come on, it sounds like a fairy tale."

"Nee, it's Gott's word to His people. Once you accept Christ and belong to Him, He helps you understand. Not everything is literal. Even Christ speaks in parables, but the message is true. I love to read it, even though some bishops discourage it. Our bishop is more liberal. He even allows cell phones."

"I know you have one, but I never see you talk on it. Why do you carry it around if no one ever calls you?"

Belinda felt a blush travel up her neck. "Someday, someone might call me."

"Oh, Belinda, it's because of Jeff, isn't it? You still think he'll call you."

Her embarrassment continued to show as scarlet rose in her cheeks. "It's silly, I guess."

"No, it's not silly. I didn't mean to upset you. But it's been a long time."

"Jah how well I know. I think Zeke is getting impatient with me. Last time we were together he tried to hold my hand."

"And?"

"I couldn't do that. I don't want to hurt him and so far, I don't feel anything for him."

"Then tell him."

"It's selfish maybe, but I keep thinking if it's never going to work with Jeff, well, Zeke is not a bad choice. In time, I'd probably learn to love him. At least I know he's a really solid Amishman and would be faithful and gut to me."

Madison shook her head. "I see. I don't blame you then. Yeah, don't burn any bridges yet. Why don't you go see Jeff and get it out once and for all? Maybe he's going with someone by now, and you're wasting your time thinking about him."

"I think I'm afraid to find out. His sister hasn't called me in ages. If he was dating, I know she'd stay away so she wouldn't have to break the news. She knows how I feel."

"But if you put your head in the sand, you can't move on."

"Mmm. I never thought of it that way. I'll think about it. Danki."

A cardinal caught their attention as he flew into a holly bush and disappeared behind branches. Lottie bounced up and down in the stroller pointing towards the bush.

Madison smiled at her sister and turned back to Belinda. "Let me know when you hear from your friend about the adoption thing. I want to know if it's even an option before I look into other possibilities."

"I'll write her tonight. I'd call, but she doesn't like phones."

"Wow, she really is Amish," Madison said, grinning.

"Jah, we Amish are peculiar people," Belinda said with a wink.

Chapter Twenty-Eight
Lancaster County, Pennsylvania

Josiah brought in an armful of sweet corn. Fortunately the drought was short-lived and the crops were booming. Tomatoes were ripening on the vine and he was about to go out to collect some for supper when he noticed Katie's expression as she sat reading a letter.

Her brows were furrowed and she had her kapp ribbons twisted about her fingers—a sure sign of stress with his Katie.

"I hope it ain't bad news, Katie," he said as he placed the ears of corn on the counter next to the sink. She looked up.

"I don't know what to call it. Can you sit a minute and I'll read it to you?"

He nodded and removed his muddied shoes before taking a seat across from her at the kitchen table.

"It's from Belinda. It reads:

'Dear Katie,

Hope you are feeling better now that you're further along in your pregnancy. I was so excited for you and Josiah. I know you wondered if you would ever find yourself in a family way, so I know you must be thrilled.

I told you about the family I sit for and I know I mentioned their young teen-age daughter, Madison. We've become quite close and she's confided in me about many things. It's a sad thing to report, but she

181

too is in a family way, though she is not married. She's not a bad person and I know she's ashamed for her behavior. I've talked to her a lot about Jesus and I'm hoping she will turn from her ways and give herself over to him.

Anyway, when she first found out she was expecting, she was sure she wanted to end it. I talked to her about her choices and she realized that a real boppli was growing inside her and it was not just a blob of tissue, which is the lie spread amongst the Englishers. When she realized, she couldn't bring herself to destroy her child and made the decision to deliver it at term, though she feels she would not be a good mother at her age and would want more for her child.

In other words, she wants to put it up for adoption. She is about five months along now. Thinking that you might not be able to have your own kinner, I had mentioned the possibility of you and Josiah adopting her child, which is a baby girl. Now, of course, I guess everything has changed and I'm so very happy for you. I know this may be the wrong thing to ask, but I'm asking it anyway since I've prayed about it so long and maybe I should.

Would you be interested in adopting her baby anyway? She should be a sweet one and very smart, since Madison is both. Actually, she's very smart (about book learning, anyway), but maybe I wouldn't call her sweet. She's getting nicer though and she means well. I'm proud of her for not destroying her baby's life and being willing to give it up for adoption. It was a difficult decision, but I believe the right one.

She lives with her father and step-mother and the situation is not good. She dislikes her step-mother and I guess it's mutual. Anyway, she wanted me to write to see if there was any possibility of you taking in her child. Please do not feel guilty in any way if you think it would be too much for you. I know your situation is difficult having to deal with leukemia at the same time. Either way, I will understand. If, however, you have any interest, Madison would want to meet you. I'm sure you would want to meet with her as well. She's getting very good care. There would be no cost to you at all. She just wants to have a loving family raise her child.

I will wait to hear from you. Nothing new with Jeff, though I still think about him a lot. Zeke still likes me and he's trying his hardest to be patient with me. More patient than I deserve.

Give your whole family my love. I miss you all.

Love, Belinda'"

Katie stared over at Josiah, who was nervously twisting his straw hat in his hands. She couldn't read his expression. Finally, he asked her what she thought about the idea of adopting.

"I don't rightly know. Now that I'm expecting, it might be just too much, yet what a wonderful opportunity to raise a dear boppli."

"Jah. I guess so. I just worry about you, Katie-girl. They'd be only a couple months apart."

"Well I had talked about twins. I guess it would be about the same."

"Do you think you could love another child as your own?"

Katie slowly nodded. "Gott has given me a whole bunch of love inside to share. There is no limit to love. How about you, Josiah? Would it be too difficult for you?"

"Nee. I love kinner, too. I love my nieces and nephews like they were my own. I think we should not decide anything until we pray about it—together and separately.

The other thing is, we need to meet this girl. Genes are important."

"Jah, true. Of course, we Amish have had our share of problems by having people marry distant relatives. You know that's not gut. This would bring fresh blood into the community."

"Would we tell her she was adopted?"

"You're getting ahead of yourself. One step at a time. I won't write back until we've given it a great deal of thought."

"And prayer."

Katie nodded. "That's most important. Gott would provide, I'm sure and certain of that. Both food and love."

"Jah. It's a shock though. I never expected to have this come to us. Funny, but I was putting out feelers all over the place before you became pregnant—hoping to find a boppli up for adoption and now this. Just landing in our laps out of the sky."

Katie laughed softly. "Maybe that's the gut Lord telling us something."

"Maybe so, Katie. We'll ponder it in our hearts. In the meantime, I'll put on water for the corn. It's perfect this year. The raccoons didn't even get to it first."

She smiled and reached for a large pot. My goodness, life can change in a heartbeat.

First she thought she was barren and now this. Thank you, Gott.

Holmes County, Ohio

Jeff threw his soiled clothing into a pile in the bathroom while he showered. He let the cool water rinse his hair longer than usual. The soil was still wet from the last thunder storm and digging holes for the half dozen peach trees on a customer's property left him, not only worn out, but filthy as well. His mother made him take off his socks and work boots on the porch before allowing him to enter the house.

He worked six days a week now, which helped with his college expenses. He still put money aside in case he married or found land at a good price, but the rest of it went to help pay off his school debts. Even though his parents helped him with his tuition, there were other expenses like books and fees to pay. It seemed every time he turned around, there was an additional charge for something.

After drying himself off, he put on his swimsuit. It had become a routine. Rise early, work all day, shower, and then take a dip in the pool. He was too beat to do many laps, but it felt good to be surrounded by fresh cool water. The past several days the temperatures had been in the high nineties. He kept drinking water all day to keep from getting dehydrated.

As he slowly swam around the perimeter of the pool, his father came out of the house with a glass of wine and sat at the round patio table to catch up on the news. He spread the newspaper out and then nodded to his son. "Ready for dinner?"

"Not yet. What's Mom making?"

"She's not going to be here tonight. She's joining some friends for dinner and a movie. Some chick flick."

"So what are you thinking? Pizza sent in?"

"That, or hot dogs on the grill. It's up to you."

"Either."

"Then we'll call for pizza delivery when you're ready."

After a few minutes, Jeff climbed out and dried himself. He sat and picked up a section of the paper and started to read when his father cleared his throat and sat back in his chair. "This might be a good time for a father-son talk, Jeff."

"Oh?" Jeff put his paper down and leaned back in his seat, folding his arms over his chest. "Is there a problem?"

"I wouldn't call it a problem exactly, but your mother and I haven't heard about your decision to go on for your bachelor's degree. You should be checking out colleges if you don't want to lose time."

"I think I'll just take the two-year program here, Dad. I appreciate your offer to help out, but I believe I'll know enough about running my business after these courses are done. I'm learning a lot on the job, too."

"You still just want to run a landscaping business? Have you considered law or engineering?"

"We've been through this before, Dad. I'm not interested in sitting everyday in an office. I need to be active physically. You know how I am."

"That's fine now while you're young, but—"

"When I'm too old to go out on the job, I should be making enough money to hire people to do the hard labor. But that's not for a long while, hopefully."

His father looked down at his hands and twisted his thumbs. "The other thing—I know you've been seeing some Mennonite girl. Are you still interested in getting involved with one of these Plain People?"

"Is there anything wrong with that? Besides, it's not serious with Megan."

"Well, I'm relieved to hear that. First it was that Amish girl, then a Mennonite. When are you going to date a girl more like yourself?"

"Maybe you don't know who I really am, Dad. I've changed about a lot of things. In fact, I haven't totally eliminated the possibility of going Amish myself."

"For Pete sake, Son. What's gotten into you with all this religious stuff? Are you on drugs or something weird?"

"I hope you're not serious. That's the last thing I'd do. Look, if you'd let me explain about the Amish and their beliefs, maybe you would understand better."

"I know all about them. They don't want anything to do with the real world. They're in some kind of cultish delusional sphere of their own making."

Jeff gritted his teeth. It was so difficult to talk to his father about it. "It isn't a cult or a fantasy. They just want to avoid the culture we live in."

"So can't they just turn off the TV when they don't like a show?"

Jeff rose from the table. "Dad, I think I'll skip the pizza. I've lost my appetite. In fact, I'm going to go see a friend."

"Just like that! You can't stay and face the truth. I'll tell you right now, no son of mine is going to make me look foolish by trotting around in some stupid buggy with a beard hanging down his front. Your mother and I can't deal with such foolishness."

Jeff stomped into the house, his heart rate doubling. *Respect your parents. Respect your parents.* It was getting harder all the time to even converse with them. Was he becoming eccentric? Maybe he was letting his love for a certain Amish girl affect his brain matter. It was time to see Belinda again. Perhaps if he saw her again, he'd see her differently—the way so many in his world would see her. Plain, foolish, old-fashioned, and strange.

He checked his watch. No point in calling first. He was sure she didn't use the cell phone any longer, though he still paid for her service, hoping someday his phone would ring. No, he'd just head over there and face the consequences. He knew her parents wouldn't be thrilled to see him. And maybe Belinda wouldn't either, but his life was going no where now. He had to know for certain if there was any hope left for them.

Though he could have walked there, he preferred the car. Black and modest, but it ran like a charm. Could he really give that up as well as everything else?

Chapter Twenty-Eight
Lancaster County, Pennsylvania

Katie sat staring out at Josiah as he and his brothers threshed the oats. He was so strong and in excellent health. If only she felt as certain of her own health. The doctor had not seemed pleased at her news when she first told him of her pregnancy, but her tests so far were good. No sign of the dreaded leukemia returning at this point. He mentioned the possibility of treatment down the road, but she feared damaging her baby. The effects of her disease if left untreated could be serious, but she would have to wait until the birth to receive medication. She was adamant.

She and Josiah prayed each night after receiving Belinda's letter. She hadn't felt like writing back yet, though she knew it was poor manners not to. She was sure the young woman would be anxious to know. Could she handle the care of two infants at the same time? Certainly under normal circumstances, it wouldn't create a problem, but there was nothing normal about her life right now. It would be ever so nice to have two kinner to love though, and no one knew if she'd be able to bear another of her own. Perhaps this was God providing a way for all concerned.

Tonight Josiah wanted to make a decision. Not a final one since they'd have to make arrangements to meet this young girl. Perhaps she would not find them to be the kind of people she would want to raise her child. Of course, if she was willing to give up her baby, maybe it wouldn't much matter. It sounded as if the girl was truly concerned about her child's future. To go through nine months and the birth, and then be willing to have the child adopted took a lot of love on the girl's part. The English world allowed for the horrors of abortion and apparently it was performed often enough to be acceptable in their eyes. How sad. How tragic indeed. When a life needs the most protection, it is endangered instead, and often terminated. How does God put up with this world?

Katie wiped a tear with her apron. Nee, it would be a privilege and an honor to take this young unwanted baby girl and give her a home. If Josiah was agreeable, she knew what her decision would be. Then the rest would be up to the young mother herself. Hopefully, she was praying about the decision as well.

That evening, before retiring for the night, she and Josiah agreed they would take the next step. Katie would write her letter the next morning. He had come to the same conclusion she had. At this point, she knew she'd be disappointed if it didn't work out, though it was still in the Lord's hands. His will be done.

Holmes County, Ohio

Jeff's hands slipped on the steering wheel from perspiration. He could blame the heat, but he knew better. His lips were dry and he had difficulty swallowing. What if that Zeke guy was there? Worse than that, what if they were already engaged? He'd look like a fool. In fact, he would be a fool. What they had felt for each other had been special, but could they go on like this forever? In limbo?

The first person he saw as he pulled in was Nellie. She was picking blueberries, loading a tin pail. She looked up and squinted, probably from the sun as it was setting behind the tree line. When she seemed to recognize him, she grinned and waved. Well at least someone was happy to see him.

After turning off the ignition, he walked over to her and shook her hand. He gave the one-shake pump, which his friend Horace had taught him. She looked surprised and let out a giggle. "Belinda's in the kitchen. You can just walk in."

He chatted a minute, asking her about the barn cats, and then walked over to the back porch. As he climbed the first step, Belinda opened the door with a bag of trash for the burn barrel. Her mouth flew open and she stopped and stared as if seeing an apparition.

"Hi Belinda." That was all he could muster.

"Jeff."

"That's me," he said, trying to sound light and casual, but it came out sounding a bit desperate.

"I was just taking the trash out."

"I can do it for you."

"We can do it together, if you want."

She stepped out on the porch and he took the trash bag from her hand. They walked slowly toward the back of the barn and neither of them spoke. The air could be cut with a scythe. Finally, after dumping the bag in the receptacle, Jeff found his voice. "I wanted to see you again. How have you been?"

"Okay. And you?"

"Not real okay, if you know what I mean."

"I'm not sure," she said as she turned to walk back to the house.

"Wait, Belinda, can we take a walk first. I want to talk to you privately."

"I guess that would be okay. My daed is busy with Gideon in the barn."

"The family well?"

"Jah. And yours?"

"They're fine." It was dusk and she nearly tripped over a rock in the path, but as he reached across for her arm to steady her, she shrugged him off. "How's the Mennonite thing going?" she finally asked.

"Good. I'm really enjoying it."

"You still enjoying the group you see after service?"

"I guess." He knew exactly where this might lead. "How about you, Belinda? Are you still seeing Zeke?"

"Sometimes."

"Let's stop here by the fence. We're out of sight and this is serious. Belinda, I can't get you off my mind. It's driving me nuts. I go to call you a couple times a day, but realize you wouldn't even answer my calls. Your parents don't want me here, my parents are against the whole idea of us being together, and now you seem to not care at all whether I'm here or not. Should I just give this whole thing up and walk away? Is that really what you want?"

Belinda began to cry. She placed her hands over her face and slumped to the ground. All the stored up tears and pain overflowed. There were no words, just sorrow. Immense, over-powering sorrow. She felt arms surround her and she leaned into Jeff's chest, accepting his embrace, drinking in his scent and his tender voice. Oh, how she'd missed him. How much she loved him.

Finally, her tears subsided and he handed her a handkerchief, which she used and then tucked into her apron pocket. "Jeff, I still care. Too, too much. I try not to, but I see your face everywhere, hear your voice—your laughter. It's been so difficult, you can't believe it, but where can we go with this? You know how much it means to me to remain with my family and community. I think it would be devastating for me to leave it all, yet…"

"I know, Belinda. It's the same for me. My father has made it clear how he feels. He's always on me about finding a girl from the club or school or anywhere but here with an Amish girl. I may have to move out. I hate the fact that I get so angry at him. I don't want our relationship ruined, but it's so hard on me. Please just give me a little more time, Belinda. Please don't find another man—not until I know whether I can become an Amishman and take you as my wife."

"You're considering jumping the fence for me?" Her eyes widened and she studied his expression.

"I am. I've been talking with an Amish guy nearly every week since we broke up, but I can't pretend to be something I'm not."

"I know that. I understand completely."

He reached for her hand and held it to his lips. "My darling. I've missed you so much. May I kiss you?"

She nodded and closed her eyes as he drew her close. They were both kneeling now on the grass and his lips felt so warm and sweet on her own. It was as if they'd never been apart.

A loud base voice broke into their perfect moment. Her father's stern, "What's going on behind my back?" jolted them back to reality. Jeff rose abruptly, but she remained on her knees, stunned by the sudden reversal of events. Her dream had become a nightmare in a split second.

"I'm sorry, Mr. Glick," she could hear Jeff say in apology. His voice wavered slightly.

"Belinda, get in the house. Now!"

She rose, nearly tripping over her long skirt, and then ran, tears streaking down her cheeks and blurring her vision, until she arrived at the kitchen door. She ran past her mother, who was stirring soup for supper, bolted up the stairs and fell across her bed, sobbing.

"I thought you were done tormenting my daughter with your tricks," Jed stated, his mouth twitching.

"Sir, I know it didn't look right, but you have to understand—"

"I understand that you have no honor. You made a promise to leave Belinda alone."

"I...I don't remember promising that. Look, we've tried to stay apart. This is the first time we've seen each other in weeks. It would be easier on me, too, if I could forget your daughter, but it's not happening. I love her. I want to marry her and she feels the same about me."

"She was getting over you. In fact, she was getting interested in a fine young Amish lad she's known all her life. That's who she should marry, not some fancy Englisher who'll tire of her after a couple years and take off."

"I would never leave her."

"You say that now, but you'd end up being ashamed of her. Thinking she wasn't gut enough or smart enough for your fancy friends. I've seen it happen."

"And if I became Amish?"

"Are you planning to?" His eyes bored into Jeff's—a challenge.

"I'm considering it very seriously."

"You don't know nothing about being Amish. It's far more than a lifestyle. It's gotta be in your genes."

"People do join from the English world. I've been taking instruction and learning about the Ordnung from an Amish friend. I just have to be sure before I take the final step. I needed to know how Belinda still felt about me."

"You can't turn Amish to impress some girl."

"I know and I wouldn't change unless I knew in my heart it was right. Believe me, I pray every day for guidance in making such a major decision."

Jed placed his fists on his waist and stood motionless for several seconds. "When you turn Amish come back and talk to me. But not before."

"Yes, sir."

"And if you ain't turning Amish, don't come around her again. Understand?"

Jeff nodded and put his hand out for a handshake. Jed looked at the outstretched arm and finally extended his own. Jeff gave the one-pump shake and then dropped Jed's hand. Jed's brows rose as he stifled a grin and then he turned his back on Jeff and walked back toward the barn.

All the way to Randy's house, Jeff thought about what had transpired. Thank God she still cared. His feelings were reinforced by her reaction and confession of love. His own feelings for her were deep and genuine. The kind a man has for his wife. *Lord, why don't you give me the go ahead to become Amish? Without Your assurance, our love is in vain.*

He pulled into Randy's drive and rested his head on his arms. *It's got to be right before you Lord or it's not going to happen.*

He took a deep breath and climbed out of his car. Thank God he had a good friend who would understand and pray for him. That was his only answer at this point. Prayer.

Chapter Twenty-Nine
Lancaster County, Pennsylvania

Leroy put his journal away when Mary joined him after supper in the sitting room. She pulled out her knitting and resumed working on a red and yellow striped scarf for Katie. She always made scarves for Christmas gifts and with such a large family, she needed to begin even in August.

"Who's that one for, Mary?" he asked as he rocked, rhythmically on the bare floor.

"Our Katie. I'm making it extra long this year so she can wrap it twice around and keep warmer."

Leroy nodded. "You take gut care of your family. Do I get one this year?"

"Oh, jah, but you're last," she said, grinning over at her husband. "Katie stopped by for a few minutes this morning. She and Becky went over to the schoolhouse to set up."

"She ain't gonna be teaching now that she's in a family way, is she?" he asked stretching his legs in front of him.

"Just till they find someone to take over."

"It'll be too much for our dochder now."

"I know. I made her promise she'd stop soon, even if they don't find someone. Becky could handle it alone if she had to. Something else she told me you might be surprised to hear." She turned her work and started knitting the next row.

"Jah? I hope it's gut news."

"I can't rightly answer that one. I'm still pondering it myself. Seems Belinda is working for a family—sitting their boppli."

"Jah, I knew that."

"Let me finish, Leroy. There's a teen in the family who is expecting a boppli and she ain't married or planning to be. Apparently, she wants to give it up for adoption."

"What's that got to do with Katie?"

"You're so impatient. I'm getting to that." Mary scowled slightly as she set her work in her basket and gave Leroy her full attention. "Katie and Josiah are thinking of adopting it. It's a little maed."

"They know it's a girl already?"

"Oh, jah, they have ways."

"For goodness sake, that would be two boppli at one time."

"Leroy, lots of girls have twins and they manage."

"But our Katie's health—"

"Jah, that's what troubles me, too. When I mentioned it, she just shrugged. I think she's excited about the idea. You know, she may not have more of her own if the leukemia pops its head up again. It could be too dangerous."

"So far, so gut though, right?" He asked creasing his brow.

"So far, but she ain't that far along. I'll tell you the truth Leroy, I wish she hadn't gotten pregnant. I'm kinda scared, truth be told."

Leroy rose from the rocker and sat next to Mary on the sofa. He placed his arm around her shoulder and squeezed it gently. "We have to trust in Gott. His will will be done, no matter what."

Mary nodded and took a slow breath. "I pray all the time."

"I know. So do I. It's hard not to be concerned."

"What we think about the adoption doesn't matter that much. She just wanted us to know about the possibility. She wrote back already to Belinda and they hope to go visit the girl in Ohio, unless they decide to come here first. Apparently the girl drives."

"Sounds like it's a rich family. Why don't they raise the kinner themselves?"

"I don't have all the answers, Leroy. We'll learn more when Katie tells us."

"And you let her think it was a wise decision?"

"I didn't make my feelings known to her at all. I wanted to ponder it and talk it out with you before offering any advice."

"Gut idea. We'll pray about it before we open our mouths. Too often we speak before our brains have a chance to sort things out."

"That's what I thought, too."

He stood and stretched his arms. "Aching today. We've done a lot of hard work lately. Might head for bed. Wayne out tonight?"

"Jah. He said he was going over to the Hosteller's to visit with the family."

Leroy laughed aloud. "To see their dochder, you mean."

Mary winked. "Jah, that's for sure. I think he likes Becky more than a little."

"We'll never hear till he's ready to pop the question."

"I hope it's soon. He's young yet, but I'd like to see him settle down a little."

"Jah. He's quite the one for flirting with the girls."

"Like his daed before him?" Mary said, tilting her head.

"Maybe. Let's head to bed Mary. I feel like flirting."

She giggled as she rose and took his hand. They turned down the wick and headed for the staircase. "Is that what they call it now?"

He pressed her hand and smiled as he nodded. "That's what I call it, honey."

Holmes County, Ohio

Belinda and Madison reclined on the patio and watched Lottie as she sat on a blanket under the shade of an awning. She had taught herself to crawl though it was slow going, which made Belinda's job easier. It wouldn't be long before it would be a challenge to keep up with the future toddler.

"You're awful quiet," Madison said as she sipped lemonade from a tall frosted glass.

"Jah. I know." Belinda's mouth drooped as she avoided her friend's stare.

"So, what's wrong? I tell you everything…"

Belinda let out a long sigh. "It's Jeff."

"Still miss him?"

"He came by yesterday."

"Really? But it wasn't good?"

"Oh, Madison, he still loves me. I was so thrilled at first."

"And then?"

"Then my father caught us kissing. He had a fit and chased Jeff away."

"No way."

"Yes way. You should have seen him. His face was as red as our Jersey tomatoes. I was afraid he'd have a stroke."

"Wow! What does he have against Jeff?"

"Just that he ain't one of us. Daed's set against us ever marrying."

"What's the big deal?"

"I've tried to explain it before. To the Amish, it is a big deal to go against tradition."

"So why doesn't he just become Amish?"

"It's not that simple." Belinda rose and moved the crawling Lottie back on the blanket and handed her some stuffed animals. "He's weighing it in his mind, though."

"If he's too stubborn, you should go with that Zeke guy."

"I don't love Zeke. You know that."

"I know, but so what? Jeff sounds like a jerk."

"Could you become Amish for someone—just like that?"

"Good grief. Of course not. Not for anyone."

"Well?"

"I get your point. I guess it's not that easy."

Belinda shook her head. "I don't know if I'll ever see him again. I don't want to go behind my parents' backs, but that's the only way we'll ever be together."

"It's not a big deal. What they don't know, won't hurt them."

"Madison, lying *is* a big deal. Remember what I said about the commandments?"

"Oh, yeah. I forgot about that. You know what? I haven't lied as much lately. When I'm about to tell a fib—like to Deb, I think about what you said and try to word it so it isn't really a lie."

Belinda grinned. "You're getting closer anyway. Deception is still bad."

Madison laughed. "I guess so. Hey, I read a Psalm last night before I went to bed. It's pretty sounding. They wrote real well back then."

"They had help from the Holy Spirit."

"Oh that. Want some more lemonade?" She lifted the pitcher and held it in the air, waiting for an answer.

"Nee. Thanks anyway."

"I shouldn't drink so much. I have to pee all the time."

"It's gut for you to have liquids, especially in this heat."

"The time drags. Did you hear back from Katie?"

Lottie headed off the blanket again toward the edge of the patio. The grass was lush from the extra rains, so instead of returning her to the blanket, Belinda followed her onto the lawn area and then squatted next to her and watched to make sure the baby didn't put grass in her mouth.

She looked over and finally answered. "Not yet."

"I bet she won't want to. I don't know what I'll do if she says no."

"What did the doctor say?"

"Dad talked to him about it while I was changing. I guess he's got connections. I don't know."

"And your parents are still not happy about Amish raising your baby?"

"They'll never be happy about that—or anything else when it comes to me. I hate it at home. If it weren't for Lottie, I'd be out of here."

"It would be hard to leave her. She's so cute."

"I bet you'll have a hard time quitting some day."

"Oh, jah. That's for sure. The way things are going with Jeff, I may be here a long time."

"He'll come around. If not, you always have that Zeke guy. I bet you'll be married within a year or two."

"I hope so."

"Of course you're only nineteen. I'm never getting married." Madison lowered the chaise lounge, laid back and placed her arm over her eyes.

"I bet you will some day. What about Cab? Do you ever hear from him?"

"No, and good riddance. I hope I never see him again."

"What about school?"

"I've decided not to go back. I'll get my GED after the baby comes and then I'll get a job and move out."

"Does your father know your plans?"

"No. He doesn't have to."

"You're only sixteen. Don't you have to be under his authority till you're eighteen or something?"

"Legally, I suppose, but he'll be glad to be rid of me. Deb will be ecstatic."

"I feel so bad for you. Maybe you can live with us if that happens."

Madison lowered her arm and turned her head towards Belinda, her brows raised. "Serious?"

"I'd have to check with my parents, but they liked you when they met you and they feel bad about your situation."

"Gosh, maybe I'll be Amish. They seem like real good people."

"You're kidding, right?"

Madison laughed. "Fraid so. I couldn't dress like you. Sorry I don't mean to offend you, it's just not my thing."

It was Belinda's turn to laugh. "Jeff's sister Carrie used to dress me in her fancy clothes. I have to admit, it was kind of fun, except I didn't like the guys looking at me the way they did."

"You're a riot. I couldn't give up my tech stuff either. I love my computer and music and phone and—everything. TV, movies, concerts—"

"I guess I won't teach you the Ordnung then," Belinda said, grinning. "You have no idea how many rules we have."

"Ugh. Why don't you become Presbyterian or something easy."

"I'm Amish, through and through. That's why this whole business with Jeff is so hard. I don't know why Gott brought him into my life to begin with."

"That's way beyond me. You know, when I pray, which isn't every day, I like the feeling I get. Like peaceful or something."

"It's gut to pray. Gott will give you peace."

"Yeah, I remember you saying that. Maybe He is real. I'm kinda thinking different about all that religion stuff. I haven't forgotten about the repent thing, but I'm not quite ready. Maybe I never will be."

"I pray for you everyday, Madison, and I'm praying you will be ready someday—and soon—to make a commitment."

"Well, we'd better go get some lunch before I pass out. I'm always hungry now. I'll be the size of a house by the time I have this kid."

Belinda lifted Lottie into her arms and followed Madison into the house.

Chapter Thirty
Lancaster County, Pennsylvania

Becky filled Wayne's coffee mug for the third time and passed the plate with the remaining brownie on it. "More?"

"May as well finish them up for you."

Becky's mother turned and smiled at her daughter's friend. "There's always more where they came from, Wayne. Becky loves to bake. Don't you, honey?"

"Oh jah."

"Danki, Mrs. Hosteller. They sure are gut."

"I'm going to play checkers with your daed in the sitting room. You two want to come in there with us?"

"Uh, I think I'll clean up in here first, Mamm," Becky said, glancing over at Wayne, who appeared not too thrilled with the mother's suggestion.

"Well, I'll be in and out, so I'll see you before you leave, Wayne," she added making it obvious that they were not really going to be alone.

Becky licked her lips and sat down to wait for Wayne to finish his brownie. This one took longer for him to devour and she figured it was purposeful on his part. He looked so adorable. Oh, how she loved him. If only he felt the same.

He looked over and grinned. "Wish there was a way we could be alone. I mean really alone."

"Oh yah? What would you do if we were that alone?" she teased.

"I think you know."

"You know some things are off limit, Mr. Zook."

"Oh jah. You've made that very clear, Miss Hosteller."
He took a tiny bite of the remaining brownie. "I want to
take you into Lancaster again. This time we can plan a
picnic at the same time."

"It doesn't have to be all the way to Lancaster, does
it?"

"Nee. In fact, we had a nice time at the creek. Wanna
go there tomorrow? I know you'll be starting your teaching
soon."

"Tomorrow? I guess that's okay. I'll check with my
mamm first though. We have to put up tomatoes."

"Everyday?"

"There are a lot this year."

"Can you just take an hour away—or two, maybe?"

She smiled and felt her heart quicken. She'd work all
through the night to get the time off to be with Wayne
alone.

Before he left for the evening, she got permission from
her mother to have the whole afternoon off, but then she
mentioned Becky's younger sister, Delores, might want to
go along. Becky noticed Wayne's expression change, but
he wagged his head in agreement. Fortunately, Delores
liked to fish, so she could be busy and leave them to
themselves. It wasn't ideal, but it was better than nothing,
that was for certain.

The next day, after filling a basket with sandwiches,
fruits and desserts, Wayne appeared and the three of them
took off by foot for the creek. Delores lugged some of her
fishing gear along and Wayne helped by carrying the food
basket and three rods, though Becky had whispered in his
ear before they left, that she detested fishing.

Delores, who was twelve, kept up a constant banter,
which satisfied Becky since she could concentrate on her
steps through the woods. If anything, she didn't want to
appear clumsy. She made sure she had a spotless apron on

over her dress and her hair was tidily twisted under her kapp.

Once they got to the spot for their lunch, Becky set everything up while Wayne helped her sister with her equipment. Becky noticed he located the gear just out of their view and she smiled to herself. Delores decided to fish for awhile before eating her own lunch, which left Wayne and Becky time to be alone. After devouring two large egg salad sandwiches, Wayne rested back on the blanket and placed his hands behind his head. "Pretty gut sandwiches. Danki."

"Anytime," Becky said and sat next to him, arranging her skirt to cover her legs.

They were quiet for a few minutes before he reached for her hand and told her to rest next to him. She didn't allow her body to touch his, with the exception of the hands, which remained clasped.

"So Becky, you thought about getting married yet?"

Did she hear right? Mercy! "Uh, it's crossed my mind on occasion."

"Anyone picked out yet?"

"Um. Why do you ask?"

"I have someone all picked out. So I wondered about you."

Her heart dropped. So they were just friends after all. He needed someone to confide in, she guessed.

"I haven't given it that much thought," she said, hoping that small lie wouldn't count too heavily against her.

He sat up and took her other hand in his, too. "Becky, I want to marry you. I love you."

Stars burst! Fireworks snapped in the air! Balloons tore through the sky!

"Oh, my!"

"That's all you can say?"

"I think so. I'm a wee bit shocked."

"You shouldn't be. I thought you'd figured it out by now." He grinned at her in a new way. More personal.

"I guess...I guess I didn't think it would ever really happen. You see, I love you, too, Wayne. I have for my whole life, I think."

"Oh, Becky." He moved closer and put his hand under her chin, lifted it, and leaned over to press his lips against hers. He moved back after a few moments and smiled. "You are my happiness. Please just say you'll marry me."

"Jah. I will marry you."

"When?"

"Whenever you say."

"We'll have to take our kneeling vows first. But we can do that this fall and marry in December. What do you think?"

"I think that would be ever so sweet. I can't believe this is happening."

"Neither can I. I can't believe I didn't realize how much I cared about you ages ago. I think I've always had feelings for you and just never knew what they meant. We'll keep it to ourselves, of course, though I imagine people will figure it out eventually."

"Oh jah," she said and laughed. "They usually do when they see two people together all the time."

"Hey! I got a fish! Help me Wayne!" They heard Delores's excited voice come from behind the bushes.

"I'll be right there, Dee." He leaned over and kissed Becky again, quickly this time and held his forefinger over her lips for a brief moment as if to say, be silent, and then he jumped up and went off to help his future sister-in-law.

Becky remained grinning into the air. Oh my, what a wonderful-gut day this had turned out to be. Her prayers had been answered.

Holmes County, Ohio

When Belinda arrived home from baby-sitting the next afternoon, there was a letter from Katie resting on her bed. She read it and was delighted that they were considering the adoption and wanted to take it to the next step, which meant meeting with Madison. Katie suggested in the letter that they discuss arrangements to meet over the phone on the Saturday coming up. Two more days. Katie planned to call Belinda from Gabe's phone around noon.

Friday morning Belinda went to the Fortina's house with the letter in her pocket, alongside her cell phone, which was forty percent charged. Just in case Jeff decided to call, she pushed the lever to raise the ring so she'd definitely hear it. It had been three days since Jeff had shown up at her farm. Three very long days. Why hadn't he called? Perhaps he was waiting for her to make the phone call. Though it was comforting to know he still cared, nothing had been solved. Her future was as uncertain as ever. Though she'd told Madison a man couldn't just change his religion because he loved a girl of a different faith, she wasn't sure she truly believed it in her heart.

Yet, it could have gone the other way. He might be thinking she should be able to meet him half way if she really loved him. The Mennonite religion seemed to be a half-way point. If only her bishop wasn't so glued to the old way of thinking. She had heard of combination marriages that had worked out for both parties. It didn't seem fair that she was stuck in this predicament.

When Madison heard about Katie's interest, she was delighted and suggested they try to get together Sunday afternoon. She was willing to drive the distance, but would have to get her parent's permission to drive that far. Even though she had her own car now, they wanted to know her every move. Another reason to move out as soon as possible. If she told them the real reason for being gone overnight, they would have refused. They showed no interest in her idea of having the baby raised in an Amish home. But it was her baby, after all. She'd make up a white lie and tell them she was planning to stay with a friend an hour away and didn't want to drive home at night.

Belinda was willing to go with her Sunday, though she had hoped she might be able to see Jeff first.

Around two o'clock her phone rang. Lottie was sound asleep and Madison was with Vera, probably gossiping about Deb. When Belinda heard Jeff's voice, she was elated.

"Honey, I have Sunday off," he started saying. "Let's get together for awhile in the afternoon. Maybe we can just meet at the covered bridge near you."

Belinda's spirits dropped as she explained her mission to drive to Lancaster County with Madison.

"Then how about this afternoon instead. I'm working till three, but maybe you can find an excuse to get away."

"I wish I didn't feel so guilty," Belinda said.

"I know. It's not the way I want things to be, but I have to see you. We're going to figure something out so we can be together. We may both have to give something up, but we were made to live our lives as husband and wife. I mean, look at us. We've tried everything to get over each other and if anything, I care more than ever. I hope I speak for you, too."

"You do, Jeff. You know that. You're right. Okay, I'll be at the bridge by three. I won't be able to stay long, but at least we can spend a few minutes together. I hear Lottie crying. She just went down for her nap. I hope she's okay. I'd better go."

"Okay. Three o'clock. If anything changes, call me. Are you keeping your phone charged up?"

"Jah. Now I am."

"Good. I love you, sweetheart."

"Jah, me, too."

By the time she reached Lottie's side, she was screaming. Her little face was beet-red and real tears rolled down her face. "Oh, sweetie, I'm sorry. What's wrong? Do you feel okay?" Belinda held her closely and patted her back. She loved this child with all her heart and grieved when she cried so vehemently.

Suddenly, Lottie vomited down Belinda's shoulder and back. It seemed to help since she was soon able to stop crying. Belinda wiped off Lottie's mouth and then rested her in the crib while she wiped herself off. Madison appeared at the nursery door and when she saw what had happened, she picked Lottie up to soothe her while Belinda went into the bathroom to dampen a washcloth for Lottie's neck and arms, which had been covered as well with the foul-smelling vomit.

Madison followed her into the bathroom with Lottie in her arms. "She feels hot, Belinda. What do you think? Does she have a fever?"

Belinda reached over and felt Lottie's cheeks, which were bright red, and then the back of her neck. "She does feel feverish. I'll take her temperature in a minute. Hold her if you will while I find the thermometer."

Madison did as she suggested and after Belinda inserted the thermometer in Lottie's ear, she read it. "Jah, it's a hundred and two. I think I should call your father."

"I'll call him." She passed Lottie over to Belinda and reached for her cell-phone. After she got off, she told Belinda he was going to have Deb come home early. "She doesn't have any clients this afternoon, but he does. He said to just keep the baby hydrated. Can you stay till the witch gets home? I'd be scared to be by myself with a sick kid."

"Sure, I'll stay." Hopefully, Mrs. Fortina would be along shortly. It would be irresponsible to leave Lottie till she arrived. After all, she was in charge and Madison was clearly lacking in baby-sitting skills. Funny, she was only three years older than Madison, but she felt they were a generation apart.

Lottie began crying again and Belinda held her gently in her arms, wiping her face and head with cool water and offering her sips of water in her bottle. She felt hotter, but Belinda rocked with her and soon the baby fell asleep. Madison sat on the floor next to the rocker and once in a while patted her sister when she woke up. Fear showed in her eyes and Belinda realized she was too inexperienced and immature to handle the raising of her baby. Madison had made the correct decision. Hopefully it would all work out.

It was ten minutes to three and Deb had not yet arrived home. Belinda reached into her pocket and texted Jeff about her inability to make it by three. He texted back and they communicated for several minutes. It was four thirty before Deb arrived home. By then, Belinda would be expected home. She and Jeff made arrangements to meet on Saturday instead. He didn't sound happy about the situation, but what could she do? Her place was with Lottie. Certainly he'd understand.

Chapter Thirty-One
Holmes County, Ohio

Saturday, a major rainstorm hit the entire eastern section of Ohio. There were warnings of high winds and possible flooding. Belinda made her way into the basement with jars of tomato paste to store and then texted Jeff about postponing their meeting. He called her right back and she was glad she had her cell on vibrate, since Nellie came down at the same time to place some more of the canned tomatoes on the storage shelves. Belinda remained in the basement and used a dust cloth to wipe down the shelves as an excuse to be there. Nellie commented about all the work she had to do and then went back upstairs.

Belinda called him back and whispered to him about their cancelled meeting. "I figured it was off when I saw the downpour," he said, his voice registering regret. "And tomorrow, you're headed to Lancaster?"

"Jah. I got permission to stay overnight. Lottie is still sick so her mother is staying home with her till she's better."

"Poor kid. I hope you don't get it."

"I feel fine. I miss you though."

"Call me when you get back and we'll try again to get together. Even an hour is better than nothing. Wish I was going with you."

"Me too. It will be nice to see everyone though. I bet the twins will seem big."

"Probably. Gotta go, honey. My boss is looking for me. Have a safe trip. I love you."

"Love you, too. Bye." She shoved the phone back in her apron pocket and made her way upstairs just as a clap of thunder seemed to shake the foundation. The lightning came almost simultaneously. It was too close for comfort. Belinda had always been frightened by thunderstorms and this was no exception.

The next day, the sky was brilliant. Clear and as blue as the pictures of the Caribbean Sea she'd seen when she was passing a travel agency one day. It was one of her secret dreams—to one day travel to see the Caribbean in person. Chances were slim that it would ever happen, but she had her dreams. Jah, no one could take away a person's dreams.

The next morning, Madison showed up at the door at six o'clock. Everyone greeted her and then Belinda took her overnight bag and a toot of sandwiches for the trip, kissed her family and got in the passenger seat. Madison took off and headed for the highway, travelling above the speed limit. Belinda felt perspiration form under her arms as she watched the countryside zap past like a speeding train! She couldn't take it any longer. "Please, Madison, slow down. You'll get a speeding ticket—or get us killed!"

"Oh, sorry. I didn't realize I was going so fast." She slowed down considerably and turned the air conditioning even cooler. "You look hot. You're sweating."

"Not from the temperature," Belinda said, trying to smile.

"Wow! I guess you're not used to cars. I was only going about eighty."

"Only? Goodness girl, you won't live to have this boppli."

Madison laughed and asked Belinda if she wanted to hear music on the radio. When she mentioned she'd like to, Madison found a station with Christian music playing, which pleased Belinda. She probably wouldn't have thought to do that a month earlier. Madison showed signs of consideration for others more all the time, even talking less hatefully about her step-mother. Belinda truly believed the Spirit of God was working. Perhaps an answer to her many prayers.

They stopped several times to use the public facilities, mainly due to Madison's frequent need to use the rest room. Madison insisted on treating Belinda to a quick lunch, though secretly Belinda would have preferred eating her homemade bologna sandwich.

Mid afternoon, they arrived at Katie's house. She was picking parsley from her herb garden when they pulled in. She waved and pointed to a parking spot by the barn. Katie walked over to hug Belinda and then turned to Madison, who at first merely held out her hand for a handshake. Katie smiled, ignored the extended hand, and reached over to give Madison a hug. Madison visually relaxed at Katie's warm welcome and grinned back at her.

After they got their luggage from the car, the girls followed Katie into the kitchen through the back door. Josiah came in briefly from the barn where he was tending to the animals. After he gave a hearty welcome, he returned to the barn.

There were many chores to attend to. He now had a dozen cows, two goats, and one steer. Of course, they had a couple dozen chickens that needed attention, not to mention the half dozen work horses. He had used money from their wedding as well as the money he had saved over the years. Katie was pleased that she had found such a competent young man who knew how to manage money as well as he did.

The girls sat down around the kitchen table as Katie served homemade molasses cookies with iced tea. She and Belinda discussed all the members of both Amish families, including Hannah's new addition and several other new boppli born in their communities since they were together.

Then Katie turned her attention to Madison, who was intent upon remembering the names of the immediate family members mentioned.

"So I understand you want to carry your baby to term, but because of your situation, you won't someone to adopt her."

"That's pretty much it," Madison said.

Katie continued. "Belinda said you're thinking about placing the child with an Amish family."

"Right again." Madison avoided Katie's eyes and looked down at her napkin, folding it into pleats.

"My husband and I have talked and prayed about it at length, and we would be happy to help out if you decide we'd be the ones you'd want to raise it. I can promise you this. If you decide to let us adopt, we would love it like our own. Josiah and I both love kinner—children, and I guess you know I'm expecting myself."

Madison looked up. "Belinda told me. She told me about your health problems, too. I'm sorry."

"Danki, but I'm doing pretty gut now. I think that Gott is going to see me through this and everything will be just fine."

"You look good," Madison said with a faint smile.

"Jah, well. Looks can be misleading. I never looked as bad as I felt, but that's behind me, Gott willing, and I will be cancer-free from now on."

"My parents wouldn't be thrilled with the idea of my baby being raised by Amish," Madison said, softly. "But it's my choice in the end."

"Is it because we seem so old-fashioned to them?"

"I guess. They think you're all a bit wacko. Oh, sorry, I didn't mean to offend you," she added as she saw Katie's brows rise and her mouth drop open.

Katie then laughed and the girls joined her. "I guess we do look strange to others, but we have strong family ties and we hold Gott up high in our daily lives. I think if they understood us better, they might not think we're so crazy."

"Yeah, I bet you're right. I've gotten to know a lot about Amish because of Belinda. She's talked to me about her life and it doesn't seem that nuts anymore. In fact, I like the way you take care of each other and look out for those who need help. Even the way you'd be willing to raise my baby. That's pretty neat. My own parents don't even want to do that."

"That's a shame. My husband is nervous about one thing though. We'd have to have everything in writing because it would have to be final. We don't want to raise your baby and in a couple years have you come back and want to take it away from us. It happens sometimes, you know."

"It won't. I know that wouldn't be right. I wonder though, if you'd let me come see her from time to time. She wouldn't have to know I was her mother, but I can't imagine never, ever seeing her again. I cry when I think that could happen." Her eyes filled as she spoke and Katie reached across the table and laid her hand on hers.

"We could work that out, just as long as we knew you wouldn't be separating us from our new dochder. Sorry—I mean, daughter."

"My father is an attorney. He could write something up legal-like."

"That would be gut."

Katie studied Madison's expression when she continued. "What about the father?"

Madison frowned as she wiped her eyes with a tissue from her purse. "What about him?"

"Does he know about the boppli?"

"No, and he never will, as far as I'm concerned."

"Can you really keep it a secret from him forever? Shouldn't you get his permission as well to have the baby put up for adoption?"

"Golly, I don't know. He definitely wouldn't care. That much I'm sure of, but legally, I guess I should check with Dad."

"Jah, that would be a gut idea. Strange things can happen and it would be heart-breaking for everyone if he tried to take the baby away from its new family—whoever they may end up being."

Belinda had been silent throughout their discussion. Now she looked over at Katie. "Can you manage two boppli at once? They'd only be a couple months apart."

"Jah, I could handle it. I'm sure. I'm ever so strong now. I've been in remission a while and I'm almost four months along and the nausea is gone." Katie looked over at Madison. "You're still not showing much. Do you have a due-date?"

"Not exact, because I forgot to mark my calendar, but the doctor figures around Christmas time."

"Ah. It will be a special Christmas." Katie patted her own abdomen, which was only slightly swollen. "Will you stay home with your parents till after the birth?"

"If I have to. I can't stand it there though. Belinda will tell you. My father married a witch."

Katie's eyes nearly popped out of her head.

"Madison giggled when she saw her reaction. "Just kidding. She's not really a witch. Just a miserable human being. She can't stand me and everyday she makes some nasty comment about me and my morals. Like she's so hot. I think she and my father were fooling around even when he was still married to my mother."

Katie shook her head in disapproval. "That's a shame. Maybe you should come here and stay with us till the baby arrives. We have a real fine mid-wife nearby."

"Good grief! My father would have a conniption if I wasn't being delivered by the head of obstetrics in a big hospital. But thanks for the offer. That's really nice of you."

"Just keep it in the back of your mind if things don't work out at home. Our midwife has delivered hundreds of boppli. Believe me, she knows more than most doctors."

Belinda nodded. "I wouldn't want a man to deliver my babies."

"Oh, I don't think anything of it. Neither do they. I guess you're just used to having a mid-wife instead."

"Jah," Katie said. "You're right about that. We have our customs, that's for sure." She looked at the clock on the wall. "I hope you're getting hungry. I made potato soup and rye bread for supper. Plus fresh blueberry pie for dessert."

"Wow! Yummy! Maybe I will move in," Madison said with a grin.

Chapter Thirty-Two
Holmes County, Ohio

"They're back," Nellie called out to her parents, who were taking a break on the back porch when they heard car tires crunching on the drive as it made its way towards the barn.

After a short conversation about trivial things, Madison took off for her home, leaving Belinda with her family. She joined the others on the porch and Nellie showed her a potholder she was making. "I'm saving it for you when you get married," she added.

Grace looked over at Jed, who had a frown on his face.

"So how was Katie?" Grace asked to change the subject.

"Gut. She looks just fine. You can't even tell she's expecting."

"Too early yet. Do you think she and Madison liked each other?" Grace asked.

"They seemed to. Katie even offered to have her come live with them. I guess she'd have to talk it over with Josiah first, though."

"I would hope so. That's a big move."

"Madison didn't like the idea of having a mid-wife deliver the boppli."

"She could always go to Lancaster."

"We didn't think of that. It's okay. I think Madison will stay on at her home. She doesn't like the thought of moving so far from her baby sister."

"Huh. And maybe her daed, too," Jed said. He sat back in his wicker chair.

"Maybe. I know she really loves her daed a lot. It's just her step-mother she doesn't like."

"Too bad," Grace said.

Belinda told them about the legal parts of the adoption and how Katie wanted to be protected from having the child taken away at a later date. Her parents agreed it would be wise to take all precautions.

Belinda was tired from the long drive and after cleaning up from supper, she went up to her room. Her phone was nearly out of power, but she saw she had a text from Jeff. It read, "I love you. Can't wait to see you. Tomorrow?"

"Yes," she wrote back. "I'm not working. Anytime."

He texted back several minutes later. "Noon at the bridge. I have off all day."

"I'll be there—God willing."

She prepared for bed and went to sleep with a smile on her face. Less than eighteen hours and she'd be with the man of her dreams.

Lancaster County, Pennsylvania

Becky brought one of the new text books she was planning to use this year over to Katie's place. They sat at a picnic table under an elm tree in the back yard as Katie husked corn for their main meal. She invited Becky to stay. They discussed the adoption possibilities and then Becky confided in her about Wayne's proposal.

"Oh, Becky, I'm so excited for you—and for me! We're going to be sisters-in-law!"

Katie laid the last ear of corn on a platter and sat back against the tree. "When is the date of the wedding?"

"We didn't set an actual date, but it will probably be in December. That's what your brudder wants, anyway. We're going for instruction for our vows right away."

"It took him a while to come around, but I knew someday it would happen."

"Nee, you didn't really," Becky said with a lopsided grin. "We had to work hard to get him to even notice me. I'm sick of making brownies," she said with a chuckle.

"That's the way to Wayne's heart—through his stomach."

"Like most men."

"Not Josiah. I wasn't that gut a cook in the beginning. I had a couple things I made okay, but I've had to learn a lot."

"Your mamm is a gut cook. Didn't you watch her?"

"Jah, but you know. If you're not actually doing the cooking, you don't pay much attention."

"True. What about the teaching, Katie? I know you can't teach the whole year."

"Nee. You'll have to look for someone and soon, Becky. Josiah wants me to stay home. He's afraid it will be too much for me to teach too."

"Jah. I understand."

"What about Leona Miller? She's sixteen I think, and she has so many sisters, she could probably work outside the home."

"I never thought of her. She'd be gut. We get along when we're together. She's so sweet and smart, too. I'll ask her. Can you believe it? School starts in only two weeks!"

"Of course if she can't, I'll come in until you find someone."

"Danki, Kate. I appreciate that. There will be about thirty kinner this year. That's a lot for one teacher."

"Jah, especially with some of those boys."

"The biggest trouble-makers are done schooling, thank the Lord."

"Oh jah. Thank Him indeed. Let's set up for dinner. I'm starving. I'm hungry all the time now."

"Goodness, what if you have twins? That, and adopting the Englisher's?"

"That, my dear friend, would be a nightmare." Katie linked her arm with her friend's and they went in to prepare dinner. Becky carried the basket with corn in her other hand. She couldn't wait for their meal. Nothing tasted better than fresh corn-on-the-cob with globs of freshly churned butter.

After the three of them ate together, Becky insisted on doing the clean-up. Katie eventually relented and allowed her friend to wash the dishes and pots, but she picked up a fresh dishtowel to dry them.

"How is your grossmammi?" Becky asked as she scrubbed a pot.

"She looked frailer than normal last time I saw her, though she's in the dawdi haus now, you know."

"Jah, I remember. That's quite a step. How are her spirits?"

"Ever so gut and Mamm is healthier than she's been in a long time. She and Daed want to travel to see one of Daed's cousins in Indiana next month. He just spent a month in the hospital. Had a farming accident, but he's going to be okay."

"Who would stay with Oma?"

"I want her to come stay here with us, but she's balking already. She wants to stay in her own place."

"That's not a gut idea. She could fall and she'd be alone."

"Actually, Wayne would be there and my older bruders live right next door, so it could be done, but I thought it would be fun to have her stay with us. Ruthie wants her to go with them, but she's so busy with her little ones, I think it would be better if she stayed with Josiah and me."

"I hope it works out for you to have her stay with you then. I can't wait to get married and I hope you won't be too busy with the adopted boppli to make it to our wedding. After all, you are my very best friend."

"I'll be there, even if the baby's only brand new. Remember Ruthie?"

"That was amazing! What a day that was."

"Oh, Becky, it was the most wonderful-gut day of my life. I hope you and Wayne will be as happy as we are."

"Me, too, Katie. I hope I never disappoint him."

"I have to get off my feet. Let's sit awhile before you leave. I want to hear all about Wayne's proposal and everything he did."

"Maybe not everything," Becky said as she winked at her friend.

"Did he kiss you again?" Katie asked as they sat down in the living room.

"Mmm. And he's so sweet about it. I'm afraid to be alone with him too much, though. I want everything to wait until we're married."

"He understands that, I'm certain. You'll both be too busy with the harvest coming to find much time alone."

"Jah, true. I may leave in a few minutes and go over to Leona's place. It's only a couple miles away. If she accepts and the board okays it, maybe you'll only need to work for a week or so."

"Becky, that would be ever so gut. Jah, let me know what she decides. Josiah has been kind of worried about it all."

"He's a gut husband, Katie. Gott has blessed you."

"Jah, indeed. And you and Wayne will have a wonderful-gut marriage, too. I'm certain of that."

After she left, Katie picked up her crochet and worked on a baby bonnet. She held the half-finished pale yellow hat over her fist. It wouldn't be long before she'd be placing it on her own little boppli. A thrill ran through her spine as she pictured her life in only a few short months. She no longer worried about the outcome of her state of health. She felt confident in her future. That, in itself, was a blessing from the Lord. She closed her eyes and prayed a prayer of gratitude. She prayed for Madison and her unborn child. Gott was in control. So much better than trying to control your own life, she thought as she completed the crown section of the bonnet. She laid it aside and headed for bed.

Josiah followed an hour later and laid his hand over her abdomen as she slept on her back. He smiled as he pictured his life in a few years, working the land with his wife and kinner beside him. Even if they only had the two children to raise, he was ever so pleased to be granted the opportunity to be a father to them.

Within minutes, he was sound asleep. Hard work and sound morals provided a peace in his spirit.

Chapter Thirty-Three
Holmes County, Ohio

Belinda hoped her family wouldn't notice she had dressed in her newest blue frock. Normally, she saved her best clothes for Sunday, but today was special. In an hour, she'd make her way to the covered bridge to see Jeff. Her phone battery had died, so she hoped she hadn't missed any messages. When she came downstairs, her mother and Nellie were putting up more tomato puree. The temperatures were lower now, which made it more comfortable in the kitchen, though the kettles emitted high heat. They barely noticed her as she told them she was going to take an hour or so off before starting the zucchini pickles.

Jeff was already waiting for her, though she was ten minutes early when she arrived. There were no people and no vehicles when they reached each other and he took her into his arms and held her close to his chest. She closed her eyes and drank in his scents and felt safety in his embrace. Then they kissed, more passionately than they ever had before and Belinda wanted to remain in his arms forever.

Finally, they separated and he held on to one hand as they walked through the bridge to the path on the other side, which led down a country dirt road. It was one of her favorite places as a child and she often went there with her friends to play hide and seek and just to catch up on news.

"You look so pretty," Jeff said, scanning her fresh dress and apron.

"Danki. It's new. I made it last week."

"Ah. And you didn't wait for church service. That must mean something."

She laughed and nodded. "I think so. You figure it out."

"I'm flattered. You'd look wonderful to me in anything, Belinda."

They walked a few minutes in silence. Then he asked, "Have you thought anymore about becoming Mennonite?"

"Jeff, I have, but for some reason, I don't think I can do that. I don't know what we're going to do." She could feel tears forming and forced herself to remain positive and strong. "Maybe in time. I think that's what we need. Just more time. I want to talk it over again with my parents. Maybe they've softened a bit."

"I doubt your father feels any differently about it. He made that pretty clear the other day. If he knew we were together today, I don't know what he'd do."

"He can't keep us apart. It just ain't—isn't right."

"I feel the same way, but at the same time, I feel terribly guilty. It's lousy to have such mixed feelings."

"Jah, how well I know."

Belinda checked her watch. "We'd better turn around. We've been walking almost half an hour and I need to get home."

They turned and he was silent until they reached the bridge. "This isn't going to work. We need to find a solution. Let's pray about it again and meet next week at the same time here with answers."

"Mercy, that's a lot of pressure. Can't we take more time to think it through?"

"Belinda, we've had a lot of time. I'm heading over to my Amish friend's house when we say goodbye. I still have questions—unanswered—that prevent me from making a decision about changing over to Amish. Until I get answers, I'm in a quandary and it isn't fair to either of us—or to your parents. We simply can't go on like we are."

Belinda blew out a stream of air as she knitted her brows. "You're right. I'm going to weigh my options. I don't think my parents would shun me, but the rest of the community surely would. But wouldn't it be worth it, if we were married?"

"I can't answer that one for you. I'm having enough difficulty answering my own doubts and questions. This has been the toughest time of my life."

"Are you sorry we met?" Belinda studied his eyes.

"I'll never be sorry, even if…"

"Me too."

She walked to his car and leaned against the fender, her arms crossed and head down.

"Honey, don't look so sad. We'll work things out. Come let me kiss you goodbye."

She pushed herself away from the car and allowed him to surround her with his strong arms. Oh, how could she ever break up with this man?

As she watched him pull away, her heart was heavy with indecision.

When she returned to her home several minutes later, it was almost a relief to find herself busy pickling. Working, and chatting with her mother and sister in their familiar *Deitsch* gave her comfort—even if it was temporary.

Jeff hoped Horace wasn't too busy to talk to him. When he pulled up the drive, several of Horace's children were weeding and working around their gardens. They waved and Horace emerged from the barn. He grinned at Jeff and waved. After a few pleasantries, Horace asked his eldest daughter to bring iced tea out to them as they sat together on two folding chairs on the front porch. When she returned she put a tray on a small table, which included a pitcher, glasses, and two whoopee pies. The men drank some tea and took bites out of the dessert. "So anything special bringing you here today? I didn't expect to see you today."

"I know. I hope you have time to talk for a few minutes."

"Always find time to talk to a friend," he said, nodding—his beard grazing his shirt.

"I've got to make a decision one way or the other. I can't become Amish unless I'm positive it's the right way to go. I've prayed and prayed about it, but God seems silent."

Horace's lips were clamped shut and he looked past Jeff appearing to contemplate an answer before speaking. Moments passed. "Jah, sometimes Gott wants us to use the brains he supplied us with and he chust listens. What troubles you the most? Lack of a car?"

"At first that seemed paramount, but not anymore. In fact, I'm almost ready to start my own business, though it will be small at first, and I'd be working off my own land. I'm looking around for an acre or two. I've decided I could just grow trees and plantings for re-sale. Run a nursery. Maybe concentrate on wholesaling for awhile and sell off of my land. I wouldn't have to get into landscaping right away. Maybe down the road."

Horace nodded and bit off more of his whoopee pie. "You would be satisfied?"

"As long as I was working outdoors in the soil and making a living. Yes, I believe so."

"Then what else is troubling you?"

"I guess it's the fact that my family is totally against my becoming Amish. They weren't happy when I became a Mennonite and this next step kind of sets them over the edge."

"I see. And they probably think it's a cult?"

"I guess. I've tried to explain—"

"Jah, it's hard for the Englishers to understand our need to remain separate. Would they disown you?"

"I don't think it would go that far, but they certainly wouldn't include me and my wife in their social events."

"And that would be a serious problem for you?"

"Actually, no." Jeff leaned back in his chair and folded his arms. "I really could care less about the society they move in, but I love my family and I don't want to hurt them."

"Jah, that's difficult. Many people remain in the Amish faith just to avoid hurting their loved ones. Jeff, it's a tough decision to make, but I haven't heard your concerns about the theology part."

"I have no trouble with that—or even with most of the rules, though I don't honestly understand some of the reasoning that goes along with some of them."

"Yet you'd obey them?"

"Of course."

Horace smiled and nodded. "How are you doing with the Deitsch? Practicing?"

Jeff laughed. "I'm trying. It's easier for me to read than to speak, but a friend at the meetinghouse was Amish and she sometimes converses with me in your language."

"Gut. It's important. Our church services are nearly all in our language. You've attended, haven't you?"

"A couple times. I really enjoy the singing. The old hymns sound beautiful a cappella."

"Jah, some of those songs go back to the old country. They will never die."

"I have to make a decision before next week. I think it helps to talk about it. What do you think, Horace? You know me pretty well by now. Do you think I'd be a good Amishman?"

Horace pulled on his beard and his eyes gave off a sparkle. "Jah, a very gut one. I'm certain of that. But you have to be absolutely sure before you'd get further instruction for taking your vows. Once your kneeling vows take place, there ain't no turning back."

Jeff nodded. "It would be a life change that I'd never regret as long as Belinda was at my side."

"Belinda? Belinda Glick?"

Jeff realized too late he'd spoken her name. "Yes."

Horace smiled and continued to nod—his beard bobbing up and down. "Nice maed. Gut family."

Jeff discussed several other miner points about some of the rulings before he stood to leave. Horace rose and walked him to his car. They shook the one shake and Horace patted him on the shoulder. "You would be very *wilkim*, if you decide to join the Amish."

Thank you, or should I say 'danki,'" Jeff said with a smile.

"You say it any way you please. Let me know what you decide. If you want me to talk to your parents and explain anything, I'd be happy to do that."

Jeff thanked him again and said goodbye before heading home. Many of his questions were now answered. It was decision time. No matter what the final decision would be, he knew he could no longer live the way he was, deceiving both families and causing misery for not only himself, but the woman he loved, as well.

Chapter Thirty-Four
Lancaster County, Pennsylvania

Ruthie and Emma brought their children over to Katie's house for a visit one afternoon. They were having a heat spell and it was too hot to sit in the sun, though they settled on the back porch so they could watch the little ones as they played in the yard. Josiah was at one of his brother's houses to help them with the second haying.

Katie had not yet told her sisters about the pregnancy, since she wanted to be absolutely certain first. She'd sworn her mother to secrecy. As they sat drinking fresh lemonade, Emma looked over at Katie and tilted her head. "You okay?"

"Jah. Why do you ask?"

"I don't know. Just look different, is all."

Katie grinned. "Jah, I am different. I'm in a family way!"

Both her sisters looked at her, first shocked, and then elated. Ruthie patted her hand. "Just what you had hoped for, Katie. I'm thrilled for you."

"Oh, that's wonderful-gut news," Emma added. "I bet Josiah is walking on clouds."

"He is now. We were both a little overwhelmed at first. We just didn't think it would ever happen to us. Gott is gut."

"Oh, He is that," Ruthie said as Emma nodded in agreement. "So when are you due?"

"February. It seems so far away."

"Jah," Ruthie agreed, "the first one seems to take the longest. I guess cause you're not as busy."

"I have some other news."

Her sisters both stopped talking and waited.

"We're going to adopt a boppli, too."

That really shocked them. "Oh my goodness! From an agency?"

After explaining the whole story, her sisters exchanged glances. Ruthie's mouth was drawn. Then she asked her, "Is it a gut idea? I mean with your leukemia and all, won't that be too much for you?"

"We've talked about it at length. You see, I think we prayed so hard for a boppli, that Gott figured he'd give us two to love. We'll raise them like twins."

Emma shook her head. "It ain't easy, Katie. I should know."

Katie pointed over at the two little blonde girls digging in the dirt beside the porch. "And look how gut they are."

Emma giggled. "Gut? Jah, right now, but you should see them sometimes, little troublemakers."

Ruthie smiled at their exchange. "We can help you in the beginning, Katie. Don't you worry."

"Actually, I don't worry. I know Gott will give me the strength when I need it. He's gotten me through so much already in my life. I know he never leaves nor forsakes his people."

"You speak truth," Ruthie said as she nodded. "I know that for a fact, as well."

A cool breeze stirred and soon it was time for the sisters to return to their homes. Katie watched as their buggies left the lane. Her life was complete now. She touched her expanding middle and prayed for her infant's health, as well as Madison's. Then she turned to clean off the table on the porch. How blessed to have her family. How blessed to be Amish.

Holmes County, Ohio

The week passed slowly. Each evening Belinda spent time alone in her bedroom in heavy prayer. At first her mother questioned her disappearance each night immediately following the kitchen clean-up. When Belinda admitted she needed the time for personal prayer, Grace just nodded. "We could all use that, dochder. Say a prayer for me."

Tomorrow she and Jeff would meet and decisions would follow.

Belinda considered every alternative, but it kept going back to leaving the Amish for the Mennonite religion. There would be little difference as far as her beliefs, and it would certainly not be difficult to adjust to electricity and cars and phones. Nee, all those things would be plusses in her life and easy to accept. Jah, she had to do it. She could not stop loving Jeff no matter how hard she tried. When she looked at Zeke when they were at Singings or church, she never felt anything beyond friendship. How could she be intimate with a man who felt more like a brother than a mate?

It was still early evening. She could hear her parents' voices downstairs. Nellie's giggle caused her to smile. Oh, Nellie, I hope you'll forgive me. She had discussed changing over to Mennonite with her older sister, Rachel, and was surprised at her acceptance of the idea, but Nellie. Would Nellie forgive her?

After one final prayer for the Spirit to guide her decision, Belinda made her way downstairs and joined her family. Grace looked up. "You look upset, Belinda. Anything wrong?"

"Nee, or maybe jah. I don't know. I just want to talk to you all about something very important."

Jed laid his farm journal aside and sat back in his chair. Grace put her mending down and Nellie stopped working on her jigsaw puzzle and stared over at her sister. Gideon was doing a crossword puzzle, and laid it down on the floor.

"I guess…I guess I'll just start by saying that Jeff and I still love each other and want to marry."

A paper clip could be heard dropping—the room was so silent.

Belinda forged ahead, her words spilling over each other. "I know it's a problem because of our religious differences and believe me, we have been concerned about it. We never wanted to deceive anyone about our feelings. In fact, Jeff has been learning about our ways, trying to decide whether he could change over."

"Jah, and he should," her father broke in. "He knows you could be shunned. It ain't fair to expect so much from you."

"But Daed, he can't just change because of me. He needs to believe in his heart it's the right path to take. I wouldn't want it otherwise. My becoming Mennonite would be far easier on both of us."

Grace had tears streaming down her cheeks and Belinda tried her hardest not to be swayed by them, but it was so difficult. "Mamm, don't. Please don't make this any harder. I've cried buckets over my decision. We won't be banned from seeing each other. No one would do that, for heaven's sake. We would be 'black car' Mennonites and live almost the same. Our beliefs are so similar, just not so many rules to follow."

"Those rules are what separates us from the world," Jed said. "You turn your back on the Ordnung, and you turn your back on us."

Nellie hadn't said a word yet, but her eyes told of the pain she was enduring. Finally she added her thoughts. "I could never turn away from you, Belinda, I don't care what the old bishop says."

"Nellie! Shame on you for saying that."

"It's true. She's my schwester and she'll always be my schwester. No one can take that away!" Nellie jumped up from her chair and slid next to Belinda on the sofa, squeezing her around her waist until Belinda let out a cry.

"Nellie, you can't believe how relieved I am to hear you say that. I've been miserable worrying about your feelings toward me. You know I'll always love you no matter where I end up living."

"And Gideon? You won't disown me, will you?"

He looked down at the floor and shook his head. "Nee. Never."

Belinda looked over at her mother. "You will always be my mamm, even if you never want to speak to me again. And you, too, Daed," she added, as she turned her eyes to him. His eyes were glassy and it frightened her to see him show his emotions. She was breaking her daed's heart— and her own in the process.

He spoke softly. "We will always love you, Belinda. You know things will never be the same, though. You have to accept that. You won't be considered part of the community. I hope you've considered everything before making your decision."

"I have. It's not the way I would have chosen. In a way, I'm sorry I ever met Jeff, but I did and there is no going back." They sat silent for several minutes. Then Belinda rose. She went over to each of them and kissed them before turning towards the staircase. No one spoke.

When she went upstairs, she knew in her heart, it was true. Things would never be the same.

Chapter Thirty-five
Holmes County, Ohio

Belinda was preparing to walk over to the bridge to Jeff when she heard a knock on the front door. It wouldn't surprise her if it was Zeke. Sometimes he made any excuse to drop by, but today she wouldn't have time for more than a perfunctory greeting.

When she came down the stairs, the bishop was standing in the entryway. He removed his hat and nodded to her. Then he followed her daed into the sitting room. Grace and Nellie remained in the kitchen. Surely her father hadn't had time to send for the bishop already. Had word gotten out somehow? Perhaps it had absolutely nothing to do with her situation. In fact, she doubted it did, since the bishop seemed pleased to see her. Nee, maybe it was a church matter.

Belinda left the house through the kitchen. Nellie's brows arched as Grace and she peeled potatoes. "Where are you going?" Nellie asked.

"For a walk. I'll be home soon."

"You're getting out of work again."

Grace clucked her tongue. "Are you her mudder now? She works all week taking care of the boppli. Now she can take a break."

"Danki. I'll be home soon. Save the beans for me."

"We will," Nellie said, a scowl disfiguring her otherwise sweet expression.

Belinda nearly ran to the covered bridge. She was about a hundred yards away. No Jeff yet. Of course she was a bit early. She was sure he'd arrive. An Amishman was coming through the bridge, his silhouette dark against the bright background on the other side of the bridge. She couldn't recognize him, but figured she'd know him when they got closer. Hopefully, he wouldn't hang around. Jeff and she needed to speak privately and it was going to take some time.

Lo and behold, the man was Jeff! The Amishman was Jeff! Could it be? Her heart nearly jumped out of her chest. Surely, he hadn't—yet, why would he be dressed like that?

"Belinda? Don't you recognize me?"

"Jeff! Why are you dressed like…like—"

"Like an Amishman? Because my love, I am training to become one."

"Nee! It can't be!"

He laughed and took two quick strides to be beside her. He lifted her up by her waist and swirled her around in circles till she felt so dizzy, she couldn't leave her eyes open. When they stopped, he placed his arms about her and kissed her solidly on the mouth. "And now, Miss Glick, you have no excuse not to marry me."

"My goodness! Jeff, it isn't just because of me, is it?"

"No. I have to admit, you had a lot to do with my changeover, but I would not become Amish if I didn't believe it was right for me. I can't change society or the world I live in, but I can remove myself from it to some degree and what better way than to have a strong woman of faith beside me. I could never love another woman the way I love you, dearest Belinda. So accept my proposal and we'll go surprise your family."

"I was prepared to leave the Amish, Jeff. I told my parents last night that I was going to go Mennonite. They weren't happy about it, but I knew I couldn't go on without you any longer. We could still go that way, if you prefer."

"I don't, Belinda, but you can't imagine how happy it makes me to know you love me that much. Enough to turn away from all that's familiar to you, just to marry me. Wow! That's really saying something.

"I have another surprise for you," Jeff said as he led her down a short lane to a thicket. There tied to a tree was a palomino attached to a shiny new buggy. "I sold my car this morning and had enough to purchase this gorgeous buggy with only part of my savings. The owner of the horse promised he was suitable for driving a buggy, but I may let you drive us back to your place. I don't think he likes me too much. We ended up in the gutter three times before we got here."

Belinda laughed and climbed up, taking the reins in her hands. Jeff sat next to her. "Now this doesn't mean I'm letting you take over at home," he quipped. "I still plan to be the family head."

"It's fine with me. Takes a lot of pressure off me, if you are in charge."

They made their way back to Belinda's house after she made it clear to the horse that he was not the one in charge. It took a few extra minutes to convince him.

"Let's go in the front to surprise everyone," Belinda suggested as she approached the drive. After securing the buggy, they walked up to the front door. "I think the bishop is still here. He arrived just before I left," she mentioned.

"Really? Maybe I should talk to him about us."

"Nee, you need to talk to my parents first."

They knocked several times before Jed opened the door. The bishop and Gideon were standing behind him. Belinda stepped in first, followed by Jeff, who took only one step and stopped with his foot still suspended in the air, before dropping it with a clod.

"Horace?" was all he could muster.

Jed looked from Jeff to the bishop.

"You know each other?"

"Jah, we're gut friends. I believe this young man has something to tell everyone. Am I right?" he asked with a face-wide grin.

"Wow! I guess so. Mr. Glick, I'd like to marry your daughter, I'm going to be Amish, and your bishop is one of my best friends!"

Jed shook his head. "What a day! Yesterday I believed my dochder was leaving us, and today she's not only staying Amish, she's getting married to an Amishman! One already approved by the bishop! What can I say? Wilkum to the family. Grace! Nellie! Come meet the family's next bridegroom! I always said there was something I liked about you, Jeffrey. I was right. Thank the Lord—I was right!"

Made in the USA
Lexington, KY
30 April 2014